# BOUND TO
## *Her Bear*

### THE MONTANA GRIZZLIES 3

## ARIEL MARIE

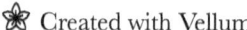

# Blurb

Drawn by her scent, bounded by fate—nothing will keep them apart.

Selen Rawlyn has a lot riding on her shoulders. As the Beta of the Brown Claw Clan, she agreed to mate with one of the daughters of a prominent clan to solidify an allegiance. She had been unsuccessful in finding her one true mate, so she would settle for one of convenience in order to help strengthen her clan.

Only the three women who were presented to her didn't interest her bear.

The scent of another did.

Rose Bell was the daughter of a powerful alpha. She wasn't considered a prized possession like her sisters, so she hid in the shadows, content with not being noticed. From the moment she saw Selen, she knew they'd belong together.

But she would have to resist.

A steel-clad contract stated the beta must choose a daughter, but it didn't include her as an option.

Selen refused to lose her mate. She would stop at nothing to claim Rose—even if that meant breaking a deal and creating a new enemy.

*If you love steamy, small town sapphic paranormal romance with a possessive bear shifter, then you will enjoy Bound to Her Bear. This story was intended for mature readers only.*

# CHAPTER ONE

"Mother, please don't start." Selen groaned. She pushed her unruly dark hair from her face. An ache was threatening to settle in her head at the thought of Bonnie Rawlyn's upcoming rant. It was one that Selene had heard multiple times, and seriously, she didn't want to hear it now. She almost wished she hadn't answered the phone, but she knew how that would have gone. Her mom would have called back to back until Selen would have been forced to answer.

Selen already had a lot on her mind, and hearing her drone on about her only daughter being mateless was not what she wanted to hear right now.

Selen Rawlyn was forty years old and didn't need a reminder that she had not found her fated mate. She—and her bear—were painfully aware of it.

The beta of the Brown Claw clan was powerful. Selen took her job seriously, and in the midst of helping her friend, the alpha, grow their clan, she had searched high and low for the one person who was to be by her side.

And so far, she'd failed.

Failure wasn't one thing Selen would settle for.

But at the moment, she was speechless at the thought that she would never actually know who fate had designed for her. Why was she not allowed to know who this person was? Selen had always felt deep in the pit of her stomach that there was one person out there for her. Was she clear on the other side of the world? Was she located in a small town in the middle of Nowhere, USA? If so, how did fate expect Selen to connect with her?

"Don't take that tone of voice with me, young lady," Bonnie sputtered on the phone.

Selen sighed and walked through her small cabin and exited the front door. The air would do her some good. Her bear paced inside her, wanting to break free and go exploring.

Selen peeked at the time on her cellphone. She'd have time to honor her bear's request. She did have somewhere to be later that day, but she had time to shift and stretch her animal's legs.

"I'm not taking any type of tone. I thought you were calling with something important." Selen immediately regretted the words the second they fell from her lips. She grimaced at the quick intake of breath on the other end of the line. Selen moved over to one of the white wooden rocking chairs that were positioned on her porch.

This was going to be a while.

"Selen Rawlyn. Discussing the future of one's mating situation is important," her mother snapped. There was no stopping Bonnie when she sank her teeth into something.

Selen leaned back and rested her boots along the railing. She might as well get comfortable for this verbal ass-chewing.

"Why is it wrong for me to want for you what your brother has?"

There it was. The comparison between Selen and her brother, Dermon. Her elder brother had found his fated mate, Suzie, and the two were madly in love with a set of rowdy seven-year-old twin boys. Selen loved her brother dearly, but she was tired of being in his shadow. One would think that Selen being a beta bear would stand for something.

Nope. All that mattered to Bonnie was that her children mated and produced cubs. Selen ran a tired hand along her face. Her mother meant well. It was obvious the fierce mama bear only wanted what was best for her children, but she was going to drive her daughter crazy with her persistence.

"Don't you think I want that, too?" Selen shot back. She was tired of having this conversation. Her ears picked up the sounds of a vehicle approaching. She felt relief at the crunch of tires traveling along the gravel toward her home.

"Well, what are you going to do about it? You can't give up. How about you come home and we throw a —"

"Absolutely not," Selen cut her mother off.

Bonnie had been trying to get Selen to come home so she could try her hand at matching her daughter off. The woman was adamant about inviting guests over for Selen to try to find her mate. There was one thing Selen knew—her mate was not in Lurton, Montana.

Their town may be small, but her mate was not hiding there. As the beta of their local clan, Selen was certain her bear would have picked up on their mate had she been there.

"What's wrong with a little party? My friend, Odessa, said there are plenty of available women in her town. We can invite some to come—"

"No," Selen replied.

A heavy sigh filled her ear. Selen's gaze locked on Eddie's approaching pickup truck, and she could have jumped for joy. She dropped her feet down from the railings and stood.

"Mom, I have to go. Eddie's here, and we have business to discuss."

Bonnie wouldn't argue with the presence of the alpha and clan business. She was the mate of a retired beta and understood that clan business was of the utmost importance. Eddie drove up to the house and parked next to Selen's SUV.

"Well, tell the alpha I said hello. We are not done with this conversation. And what is it I hear that you will be going to Chardon to meet with their alpha? What's going on?" her mom asked.

Selen rolled her eyes at the notion that her mother was aware of clan business. Somehow the gossip mill always got wind of information that wasn't to be public quite yet.

Edwina "Eddie" Fane stepped from her vehicle with the air of an alpha. She exuded power. Even Selen's bear, who exhibited strength and power, felt the alpha's presence and was ready to submit.

"I have to go," Selen reminded Bonnie who gave another one of her heavy sighs. Selen did feel slightly guilty at having to cut her off, but the woman certainly knew how to get under Selen's skin. She loved her mom dearly, but at the moment she just didn't need a reminder that she had been failing in the department of finding a mate. "I promise to call you soon."

"You do that." The call disconnected.

Selen tucked away a little reminder to call her back or she'd never hear the end of it.

"How's Bonnie doing lately?" Eddie snickered. The alpha arrived at the bottom of the stairs. Her dark hair was tied back in low ponytail. Her brown eyes were sharp and didn't miss a thing. In her hands was a folder that held documents Selen had become very familiar with.

"Driving me crazy is what she's doing." Selen slid her phone in her back pocket. She moved over to the edge of the porch and leaned against the pillar. Eddie was here for a reason. Not that she couldn't stop by to socialize, but Selen knew that Eddie had news for her.

"She's just being a mother." Eddie chuckled. "Go easy on her."

"Well, it's not like she's hounding you to just walk outside your door and find a mate out of thin air," Selen grumbled.

Bonnie didn't understand what it was like not having found a mate. Her parents were lucky. They'd grown up in the same town. Their bears identified each other as mates when they were fifteen years old. They had been together ever since. Selen wished that could have been her. Her parents were the poster board vision of fated mates.

"Believe me, I know what you are going through." Eddie's smile disappeared.

Selen swore under her breath. It had been insensitive of her to forget that Eddie was not above certain things her clan members went through. The alpha was under pressure to mate from the clan. The people they served wanted their alpha to have a mate. Eddie was not only the first female alpha of their clan, but the first single one. The elders were demanding that Eddie take a mate—be it fated or one of convenience.

"My bad, Eddie," Selen said.

The alpha shook her head and gave a slight shrug. Even with all of the pressure the woman was under, she always appeared cool and collected.

"Don't worry about it. We both have a lot riding on our shoulders," she said. She held out the folder to Selen.

"Well?" Selen arched her eyebrow. She leaned forward and took the documents from Eddie. Her hands shook slightly. She didn't know why. It wasn't the first time she'd read the papers. She knew what they entailed.

"Tom looked over the contract. If you are willing, then it will be good for the two clans," Eddie said. Her dark eyes watched Selen carefully. The alpha never missed anything.

Selen wiped her emotions from her face.

Deep inside, she wanted to wait a little longer before resorting to this, but she didn't have time.

Selen's breath caught in her throat. She opened the folder and peered inside at the contract. She had never thought she would be one to agree to a mating of convenience, but it looked as if her mother would soon be getting her way. That was why Selen didn't want to indulge her when she'd asked about her trip to Chardon. If she had let on that she was in talks with the alpha there to mate with one of his daughters, Bonnie would insist on going with her.

"I am always willing to do what is best for our people," Selen murmured. The details that lay sprawled before her started to blur. She wasn't the type of woman who understood legal jargon. That was why she had forwarded the contract to the clan's lawyers. She didn't want to go into any agreement with another clan that could potentially harm her or the people she served.

"We did add a few stipulations that I felt were necessary. We sent them over, and it would appear they have accepted them. Mondo can be a son of a bitch to work with, but he will want what is best for the Silver Fang," Eddie said.

Selen blew out a deep breath. She and Eddie had been in talks with the alpha of the Silver Fang clan. The bear shifter clan was located a few hours from Lurton over in Chardon. Mondo was a fierce alpha who was willing to work with Eddie and forge an alliance between the two clans.

The agreement would be for Selen to mate with one of his daughters to seal the allegiance. Contracts and negotiations in this day and age were common, but shifters still relied on the old-world notions of marriage—or mating—to solidify a deal.

"But you don't have to settle for a mating of convenience for the Brown Claw. We can come up with another way to work with Mondo," Eddie said softly.

Selen glanced up at her and knew deep inside that she had to do this. This alliance was needed for their people. There were many reasons why she was willing to give up her dream of finding her fated mate for a contract.

Their people needed security, resources, and the relationship they were creating with the

Silver Fang clan would be one future generations would benefit from. The Silver Fang was a prominent clan, and it would help strengthen the Brown Claw to have them in their corner.

"What could be a better show of faith to our new ally than to mate with his daughter?" she asked.

Eddie stared at her for a moment before giving a slow nod. "I do appreciate what you are doing. "Our clan will, too. This is a very honorable thing."

"You do know I was his second choice, right?" Selen joked.

Eddie snorted and folded her arms in front of her. Mondo had originally had his eyes on Eddie, but that was never on the table for discussion.

"You were going to be his only choice," Eddie said. Her dark eyes crinkled in the corners. "Are you sure you don't want me to come?"

"I'm sure. If the contract is good enough for Tom, then I'm okay with signing it," she said. She glanced at the sky and took in the position of the sun. If she hurried, she could still go for her run in her bear form, change her clothing, then head out. "I won't be going alone. Abe and Nick will be going with me."

She wasn't a fool to go into another bear's territory alone. She would take a couple of enforcers with her to be completely safe. Not that she didn't trust Mondo, but she never knew who in his clan was not on board for the alliance that was being formed. Mondo was known as a shrewd businessman and not to be taken lightly. Selen would be able to handle him. She may not be an alpha—she was a beta—and that would demand respect.

# CHAPTER TWO

"He can have one teaspoon every four hours as needed. It will help with the cough," Rose said. She smiled at the young mother who stood before her. The woman had come into Rose's shop in search of something to help her son. It hadn't taken Rose long to know what would help the child.

"Rose, you are amazing. What would we do without you?" Mona Sharp's small smile grew wide.

She had been a nervous wreck when she had first entered Rose's establishment. Now, she appeared relieved after speaking with Rose. She gathered her young cub next to her. Tommy peeked out from behind his mother's legs. The cute little tyke was four years old and just had a cold. It wasn't surprising. Even though he was a bear shifter, they still suffered from common colds, allergies and such.

Rose smiled and gave him a wave. He quickly disappeared back behind his mother's legs.

"I'm just glad I could help. I sweetened it with honey, so he shouldn't have a problem taking it," Rose whispered. She pushed the dark bottle of cough syrup she had made across the counter.

Children his age were notorious for not wanting to take medicine, but the bear shifter in him would be drawn to the honey. Cubs had a sweet tooth, and pure honey would have him wanting to take the medicine.

"Just remember, only a teaspoon. No matter how much he begs you."

"Yes, ma'am." Mona chuckled.

She bent down and hefted Tommy up in her arms. He was tall for his age, which was common for bear shifters. Most shifters, male or female, were. It came with the territory of shifting to an animal that could top out at eight to nine feet in their animal form.

"How much do I owe?"

"It's on the house." Rose folded her hands together and leaned against the counter.

There was no way she could charge Mona. The woman had almost seemed desperate when she'd come into the shop with a sick child.

"What? Absolutely not, Rose. I must pay you."

"Seriously, it's free. Take it." Rose didn't do what she did to get rich. She loved what she did. She loved foraging in the forest and woods in their territory. She had a love for herbs and plants. When she was a young girl, she'd learned how to make natural medicines and supplements. She had a gift, and it was one she took seriously. She'd opened her apothecary to help the people of her clan.

"No. I wouldn't feel right. Here's a tip then." Mona plopped some cash on the counter then snatched up the bottle and placed it in her satchel.

Rose wasn't going to argue with the woman. She smiled and took the money. She didn't even count it but slid it into her jeans back pocket.

"Call me if you have any questions." She walked from behind the counter so she could open the door for Mona.

The woman was taller than Rose who unfortunately hadn't inherited the extreme height gene as a shifter. Rose, unlike her family, was slightly taller than the average human woman at five foot nine. She was the shortest of her sisters.

"I will. I just don't know why his doctor didn't want to give us anything." Mona sighed as they walked toward the entrance of the small shop.

Rose's Apothecary wasn't much, but it was all she had. Her shop was actually popular with the people of Chardon. Humans and shifters—and even the occasional witch— frequented her business. She had made a name for herself.

"There's always going to be a difference in opinion when it comes to medical doctors and us in the natural remedies community." Rose grabbed the handle of the door and pulled it open. The chimes over the door played their musical melody. Rose offered Mona a comforting smile. "Don't worry. Tommy will be fine."

Mona gave a wave and stepped out of the door. Tommy buried his face into the crook of his mother's neck. He was such a sweet, shy boy who didn't feel good. Rose felt her heart soften at the sight.

What she wouldn't give to have a little cub to snuggle up with. She bit her lip and pushed that dream down. One day she would find her mate and settle down. When, she didn't know, but her bear, who was usually a laid-back beast, was becoming restless.

Rose took in the main road of what they considered to be downtown Chardon. It was a busy day, and the streets were bustling with people. Mona had disappeared in the crowd ambling along on the beautiful sunny day. Rose stepped back into her shop. There were a couple of other customers browsing.

She went back over to the counter where she had been working before Mona had come in. She had to finish labeling her latest concoctions she had created so she could get them out on the shelves.

Rose glanced around and felt the pride for all that she'd accomplished fill her. She had opened about six years ago, against the wishes of her father. It still hurt to think that he hadn't been supportive of her.

But then again, she wasn't truly surprised.

It was the story of her life.

Mondo Bell, the great alpha of their clan, the Silver Fang clan, had high expectations for his children. There wasn't a day that the alpha didn't push for his daughters to strive for greatness. He had wanted bears who would be smart, strong, and could be a force of nature and make him proud.

Only Rose didn't quite fit his vision of a child of the great alpha. Her sisters made him proud. Daisy, Harper, and Iris were all picture-perfect in his eyes. They were tall, drop-dead gorgeous, powerful, fierce fighters, and would be worthy as the mate of great leaders.

Rose, on the other hand, not so much. She lacked the height of her siblings, never could handle a weapon, and her bear wasn't as fierce as the other Bell daughters.

Rose was just Rose. Too bad her family couldn't accept her as she was. She had accepted the fact at an early age that she was the outcast of the family. She didn't fit in, nor did she look like them. She didn't think she was ugly, but she couldn't hold a candle to her siblings. So most of her life, she'd stayed in the shadows. The forest and woods became her safe place. Somewhere she could go and just be herself. Her love of plants was born at a time where she had no one. While her father focused on her sisters' training, she was ignored—basically forgotten.

But Rose didn't hold any ill will. Everything Mondo did, it was for their clan. He groomed her Harper, Iris, and Daisy to be worthy mates in the hopes of attracting offers from suitors where their people could benefit from other clans. Rose spent plenty of time daydreaming about her one true mate and that person coming to sweep her off her feet.

She loved the feel of the plush grass underneath her toes and the damp earth in her hands. There were plenty of days where Rose had been lost in her own world and had been in the forest for hours. When she returned home, she'd be chastised for playing outside all day.

Mondo had thought her foraging and 'playing' in the mud would never amount to anything. If he had his way, she would have been like his other three daughters.

Rose paused what she was doing and inhaled. She felt the emotions she tried to keep buried surface. She didn't want to cry in front of her customers. She rubbed her hands on her jeans and blinked a few times to ward off the tears that threatened to form. She reached for the glass jars and slid them off to the side. She moved from around the counter and decided to see if her customers needed assistance.

She dug deep and pulled out a smile she hoped was welcoming. She ambled over to Mrs. Copper who was a frequent customer.

"Mrs. Copper. Is there something I can help you with?" Rose asked.

The older woman turned from the vials she was browsing. A warm smile spread on the woman's face.

"Rose. I was looking for something to help with stress. I haven't been able to sleep at night and I just know it has to be everything going on right now. With my son and his mating ceremony coming up, Darcie just left for college, and my dear mother is sick and I haven't had the time to go visit with her."

Mrs. Copper's smile faltered. Rose's heart immediately went out to her. She rested a hand on her shoulder. She had just the item for her.

"It sounds like you have a lot on your plate right now." Rose scanned the shelf before them.

Her gaze landed on a vial that was brown with a lavender-colored label on it. She picked it up and held it out for them to look at. "This is actually new. It is great for relaxation."

"Oh, I didn't see that. What is it?" Mrs. Copper's eyes grew wide. She took the bottle from Rose and turned it to where she could read the label.

"I call it Relief. It's a tincture I crafted that has passionflower, skullcap, some oatstraw, white mulberries, and other items. It's great for tension stress and will help with sleep." Rose was confident in her tincture. She had used it on herself and had slept like a baby.

"I smell a hint of lemon." Mrs. Copper's eyes grew wide. She had opened the bottle and waved it underneath her nose.

"That nose of yours is working. I thought the lemon would help give it a nice citrus flavor."

"I'll take it." Mrs. Copper replaced the cap. Her shoulders slumped as relief filled her eyes. She took Rose's hand in hers. "I don't know what we would do without you, Rose. You have a goddess-given talent."

Rose's lips curved up into a smile. This was why she did what she did. To help people. She squeezed Mrs. Cooper's hand tight. "Thank you, ma'am."

"And aren't you closing soon? The presentation of the Bell sisters is today. Why aren't you getting dressed up?"

Rose froze in place. She was attending the presentation, but unfortunately she wasn't one of the sisters being offered up. Word had spread across town how her father had been in talks with another clan for an alliance. There would be a huge celebration to welcome the beta from the other clan.

"I'll be closing up soon," she replied. She motioned to the front of the store where her register was located. "Let me get you out of here."

R ose slid her hand along her dress with a sigh. She stepped back from her floor-length mirror in her bedroom and took in her outfit. Even though she was not one of the daughters being presented, she wanted to look her best. Her long, flowing, pale-pink dress was littered with flowers. It was a soft cotton that highlighted her shapely form, with a deep scoop neck that put her ample bosom on display. She had left her hair down along her shoulders and had only added a hint of makeup to hide her paleness.

For some strange reason she didn't feel right. The contents of her stomach weren't settling.

"What is wrong with me?" she murmured. She didn't think she was coming down with any illness. She inhaled and blew out a deep breath and felt a bit better, but something was still off. "It's all in my head."

Satisfied with her look, she spun away and snagged her sandals that waited for her by her bed. She popped them on then headed out of her bedroom and made her way through her little cabin that was located in the woods. She had left her father's home years ago when this one had become available. It had been owned by an aging member of the clan who had decided to move to be closer to her family. Rose had saved up enough money and was able to offer a fair price for it.

It wasn't much, but it was all hers. She had

taken the time to decorate it and make it a home. This was her safe place. No one would be able to bother her here. Not her father. Not her sisters. It was rare she even received company.

And she was okay with that.

It was her little piece of heaven. She had grown up being the outcast of her sisters. Being ignored was something that came naturally to her. She glanced around the open concept of the wood that made up her walls, the soft pastel colors, the fresh flowers she had picked, and was proud of the home she had created.

Rose wasn't going to wallow in self-pity. She had made something of herself, whether or not her family acknowledged her accomplishments or not, but she had. She was at least respected by the community.

Rose grabbed her satchel and placed it across her chest and exited her home. She locked the door even though there was no reported crimes or break-ins in their town. She dropped her key in her bag and began making her way to the great lodge that housed her family and where this event would be taking place.

Rose's bear grumbled, wanting to break free

and scamper around. She smiled and patted herself on her soft belly.

"Maybe later. We have an important event to go to. We must support the sisters," she murmured.

Her bear snorted at the notion. Her beast was very protective of her human counterpart and never understood why Rose didn't challenge the way her sisters treated her.

Rose was not a confrontational person—her bear was. It was crazy to think that they were complete opposites. The path she was taking to her parents' home cut through the forest which was alive with the sounds of nature and the animals that called it home. She inhaled and brought in the wonderful scents and aromas of her surroundings. It was a beautiful fall day, and she should listen to her bear. Maybe she should skip the celebration and go get lost in the woods.

No one would miss her.

Her bear sat up at the thought.

"I can't not go." She chuckled. She was a Bell, and a Bell had to be present, a unanimous front to the clan. It was her turn to snort at what her father always instilled in their family. Shaking her head, she put a little more pep in her step and hurried on.

It didn't take her long to reach the clan leader's sprawling home. Her ears picked up on the music, laughter, and conversations of the guests. The presentation was the talk of the town. Everyone was excited to hear about which Bell girl would be matched with the beta. Rose tried to not listen to all the gossip that went around town, but she couldn't help but listen when it came to this subject. Because she wasn't included, she didn't know much of anything of what was going on other than what was made public to the clan.

She paused at the mouth of the path that led to her family's home. She stood behind a wide tree and took in a caravan that had arrived. Three large SUVs drove to the front of the lodge and parked. She didn't recognize those vehicles. It must be the beta and her people. Curiosity grew inside Rose. What did the beta look like? Was she nice? Or cruel? The Brown Claw clan was known as a strong clan over in Lurton.

A tall man exited the passenger side of the second SUV. His gaze roamed at first. He must be an enforcer. Rose recognized the assessment of the area. Her father's enforcers were always aware of their surroundings. He opened the back door, and it was then Rose's breath caught in her throat. The woman who stepped from the vehicle was breathtakingly beautiful. Tall, fit with dark-brown hair left to flow along her shoulders.

It had to be the beta.

A few men gathered around her, and then they made their way toward the building. Rose didn't realize she had been holding her breath so long until she felt the screaming pain of her lungs demanding air. She didn't move until they had disappeared into the building.

That woman was going to mate with one of her sisters. Rose blinked hard at the sound of growling vibrating through the air. She glanced down at her chest and realized it was her.

Why was her bear reacting so strongly to the woman? She had never acted this way before. Rose was always in control of her animal. She took a step toward the building, but instead of entering through the front as the beta and her people had, she decided to go through the back.

Her bear slammed against her chest as if to urge her the other way. Rose shook her head, panic setting in. She couldn't believe it. There was only one reason why her bear would be behaving this way. As long as she had hoped for the day she would find the one meant for her, fate couldn't be so cruel.

Fate wouldn't show her the other half of her soul only for the woman to be here to claim one of her sisters. Tears blurred Rose's vision. She couldn't step in. As much as she wanted to, her father wouldn't stand for her to interfere. Rose paused at the back steps and fought to get control of her emotions and her animal. She blew out a deep breath and wiped the lone tear that trailed down her cheek. She would stay far away from the beta.

# CHAPTER THREE

"My daughters are fine women. Strong. Intelligent. They will make great mates to any person who is lucky enough to have them," the alpha said. Mondo Bell, a tall, broad-shouldered man with a thick mane of dark-brown hair and laser-sharp gaze. The alpha of the Silver Fang clan was known to be direct and a fierce leader.

Selen gave a nod to acknowledge his words. They were meeting privately before the presentation.

When Selen and the enforcers had arrived, they were welcomed immediately, and she was whisked away for the meeting with the Silver

Fang's alpha. Eddie had insisted that Selen traveled with more than two enforcers. Selen was a strong bear and could protect herself, but she'd humored her alpha and allowed more enforcers to go with her.

"I understand. It is a great honor to be considered worthy enough to mate with one of your daughters to solidify a bond between our two clans," Selen responded. She folded her hands together behind her back and stood to her full height. They were currently in his office with guards from both of their clans outside the door.

Selen was now grateful she had listened to her alpha. The show of force from the local clan could not be missed. Now, was it to impress her and her men, or was this how the alpha of the Silver Fang protected his people to allow them to relax and enjoy themselves? Selen had a feeling it was a little of both. A beta coming into their territory to sign a contract for a mating with the alpha's daughter, of course the man would not want him or his clan to appear weak.

Mondo stood near his impressive fireplace. The room was spacious with the decor full of dark and bold colors. The woodwork woven throughout the design gave it a rustic yet modern feel. Over the mantel was a painting of Mondo and his mate. Selen's eye was drawn to the picture. They made a handsome couple with his olive complexion and wild hair that hung past his shoulders and his mate's fair skin and pale hair that was in sweeping updo. The two were certainly opposites.

Selen's thoughts wandered to who the daughters resembled. Not that she was vain. Beauty didn't count for everything, but her curiosity was piqued. What would the woman who she was going to spend the rest of her life look like? Was she the same complexion as Mondo, or fair like her mother?

"It's not easy for a father to offer up his daughter as part of a business arrangement, but I appreciate that we are honoring the systems of our forefathers. I've researched you, Selen Rawlyn, and your family. Your name carries weight, and I appreciate the linage."

Selen gave a nod. She wouldn't expect anything else. Her family was well respected in the shifter community. She came from a long line of highly ranked men and women. From betas and alphas of clans, to the members of her family who served in the human armed forces. She was proud of the last name, Rawlyn.

"Again, sir. I find it an honor to come forth and join our two families. I'm sure we will grow close as time goes on," she said.

Mondo jerked his head in a nod.

"We need to drink to that," he muttered. At that exact moment, a knock sounded. He turned around and shouted, "Enter!"

The door opened, and a small woman with a tray in her hand appeared in the doorway. She had a tiny smile on her face and a tray that held two large pints of frothy beer. Selen held back her surprise. Beer wouldn't have been her drink of choice to toast to a new alignment with an ally, but she was going to go with the flow. She was in his territory and would abide by their customs. She just wanted to get this over with. Soon she would be presented to his daughters and would have to make a choice.

The woman stopped near Selen to allow her to take one of the chilled mugs filled to the brim. Selen appreciated a good frothy brew now and then. Her favorite drinking hole back home had the best beer on tap.

"Thank you," she murmured.

She lifted her mug from the tray and waited for Mondo to claim his. The woman gave bow of her head and scurried from the room with the door shutting silently behind her. Selen walked over to join Mondo.

"Tonight, we celebrate the union of our two clans. Of our two families." Mondo waved a hand at her. He raised his glass in the air toward hers. His dark-eyed gaze rested on her. "Here's to the Silver Fang and Brown Claw."

"Silver Fang and Brown Claw," she echoed. Selen touched her glass to his before taking a hefty sip. The taste exploded on her tongue. It was a fine brew. She glanced down at the mug. Her chest vibrated with her bear giving her approval of the drink.

"Ah, the beta appreciates the drink. It was locally brewed here in Chardon. We believe in everything local here. I'm sure we can send you home with some." His grin spread wide across his face.

Selen was impressed. She had researched the town and had learned that they believed in supporting each other. Their economy was a booming one with their town supporting all local businesses and farms. This was one of the reasons for the joining of their clans. They each had something the other needed, and together, they could grow stronger.

It was modern times, but shifters remained true to the old ways. They could have easily signed a contract and been done with it, but joining two families made it more solid. Contracts could easily be broken, but a mating between shifters could not. There was no such thing as divorce amongst their kind.

"I would appreciate that," Selen said. She took another hefty sip before turning her attention to Mondo. "I do want to thank you for opening up your home to me and my men. We do appreciate the hospitality."

They were to spend the night and return home to Lurton in the morning. Selen would have rather driven back tonight, but she didn't want to insult the alpha and her future father-in-law by declining the invitation to stay in his home. The alpha lodge was massive, and she was sure it had plenty of room for at least fifty people.

"We aim to make sure you enjoy your time here tonight, Beta," Mondo Bell boasted. "We here in Chardon love to celebrate, and tonight we certainly have a reason to. No need to worry about safety. Chardon is one of the safest towns around."

"Your hospitality is much appreciated, Alpha," she murmured.

He waved for her to move with him to his desk. She strolled alongside the bigger man. Even at her height of six foot two, she felt significantly smaller than him.

"I hope you are in agreement with what our lawyers sent over."

Negotiations were still open until they'd both signed the contract. She eyed the big man who had paused near the desk. The contract lay waiting for the two of them.

"The only thing I want to ensure that is not part of the contract is that whichever daughter you choose, I expect she will be respected, treated like a queen, and always safe under your watch." Mondo's dark eyes cut to her. There were no longer any signs of joking in the alpha's expression.

"That is one thing you will never need to question, sir," she responded. It came without question that any woman she mated with would be respected. Selen's bear was very protective and would not hesitate to defend those she cared for.

Their eyes locked steadily for a few tense moments before Mondo relaxed.

"Good. I would hate to have to come to Lurton at the distress call of one of my children. They mean the world to me," he said.

Selen didn't miss the warning in his tone. The alpha would have nothing to worry about. She still refused to back down from his stare. He must have finally seen whatever he was looking for in her gaze. He broke the stare and waved to the paperwork.

"This we will sign after you have made your choice. Do you agree?"

"That sounds like a plan," she replied. She wasn't sure why, but there was an off feeling in the base of her stomach. She took another sip of her drink. She had been feeling exceptionally well up until now. She shook it off and ignored it. Maybe it was nerves. She was about to commit to a woman she had never even known, and a lot was riding on it.

"Good." The alpha slapped her on her back. He motioned to the door. "Now that is all settled, let's go down and enjoy the festivities. My daughters should be down for the presentation soon."

Selen knocked back the rest of her beer. She set the empty mug on the desk and followed behind the big man. By the morning, her fate would be sealed to another woman. She had always imagined herself to be mated off by this age. But why all of a sudden did she have a sense of dread filling her?

# CHAPTER FOUR

"All of you look beautiful," Rose said.

She closed the door where her sisters had been finalizing their appearance before the presentation. They had gathered in one of the guest rooms. Clothing was strewn all over the room. It seemed as if a small tornado had swept through the area.

The alpha's lodge was bustling with so many of the townsfolk. Everyone was excited to know which of the Bell sisters would be chosen. There hadn't been anything like this for their clan for decades.

"Rose, I was wondering if you were going to

come and see us off," her youngest sister, Iris, said.

She turned from the floor-length mirror to eye Rose. Iris was a beautiful, with curly dark-blonde hair and curves in all the right places. Plenty of men had tried their shot at the youngest Bell sister. Iris was in a loose-flowing, off-the-shoulder dress that was hunter green and matched her eyes.

"Of course. I wanted to wish you good luck. I'm sure you are nervous," Rose said. She leaned back against the door, unsure if she should have even come. As the eldest, she figured it was expected of her, but most times her sisters never needed her.

"Luck? Ha! That beta won't be able to make up her mind. How is she going to choose between the three of us?" Harper snorted. She ran her fingers through her short blonde pixie hair and went to stand in front of the mirror that Iris had just abandoned. She'd chosen a skin-tight black dress that stopped mid-thigh. Her long legs were put on display as well as her large breasts. Harper was the second youngest and the snarkiest of the Bell children. She never bit her tongue when it came to something on her mind.

"What are you talking about? She's going to see the best woman the second her eyes land on me." Daisy barked a laugh.

Rose turned to see the second eldest of the four of them step out of the powder room. It was no surprise that Daisy was in skin-tight leather pants and a tunic that showed off her muscular physique. Daisy was known for her strength and fighting ability. She had trained with the enforcers as a teen and joined the ranks when she came of age. Harper was skilled in weaponry as well. She worked as a blacksmith in town crafting the best knives and daggers around. She was known for her craftsmanship. Iris was the artsy one of the four. Her beauty, grace, and singing voice were unmatched by anyone.

Rose sighed, wishing she was more like her sisters, but she knew that everyone was put on this planet for a reason.

"I wonder what the beta looks like? I've seen pictures of her online, but you know a person always looks different in the flesh," Iris said. She took a seat on the edge of the bed amongst the pile of clothing.

"I hear she's hot." Harper shrugged.

"Does it really matter? She's going to pick me." Daisy snickered.

The girls shared a laugh. Rose glanced around and felt out of place in their company as she always did. The three of them were close. Maybe it was because she was the eldest and older, but she was never sure why she just didn't belong amongst her sisters. They began to joke and tease on why the beta wouldn't pick each other. Rose bit her lip and took a step forward.

"I saw her," she announced.

The room fell silent, and all eyes landed on her. She reached up and tucked her thick hair behind her ear. She wasn't used to being the center of attention with her sisters.

"Well?" Iris said. She tilted her head to side with curiosity burning bright in her eyes.

"Where did you see her?" Harper asked.

"Yeah, spill it. If you've seen her, you have to tell us what she looks like? Was she ugly? Short? Fat?" Daisy barked out the questions as if she were interrogating a bad guy.

Rose swallowed hard and gave a short jerk of her head.

"I arrived a little late after closing up my shop. I had gone home so I could freshen up a bit. But when I arrived, I came down my normal path, and you know it comes out near the front of the house. The beta and her men had just arrived. She's tall and very pretty," Rose said. Her bear didn't like the fact that she was describing their mate—she blinked. Was she going to actually acknowledge the fact that her bear was claiming this woman?

Someone who she didn't know.

Someone who didn't even know she existed.

Someone who was here to claim one of her sisters.

No.

She wasn't going to go down that road. She pushed her bear back down. Her animal was going to have to forget her claim. It wasn't going to ever happen.

"And...she was just pretty? That's it?" Harper's voice broke through Rose's thoughts.

"She has thick dark hair, tall, and looks physically fit, so I wouldn't say she was fat," she continued. She glanced over at Daisy who appeared to accept that. She didn't think any of her sisters were vain enough to not be with someone if they were overweight. Rose smoothed a hand along her thighs; they had become damp with her nerves going crazy. "I could sense that she was definitely powerful. Those men were very protective of her."

Rose remembered watching the woman walk toward the house. There was an air of confidence to her. She may not be the alpha of her clan, but she definitely was the beta. Those men were on guard as if she were a queen.

"Well, that is relief. Now we have to figure out her personality. If she is good-looking, powerful, will she be a bitch?" Harped said.

"Good question. But it won't be nothing I can't handle. I'm told I can be a little bitchy." Daisy grinned.

Iris and Harper groaned while they both rolled their eyes. Even Rose had to hold back a snort. The largest of them could be downright grouchy and fierce. She could hang with the best of men and had brought a few of them to their knees in a fight.

"Aren't you a bit nervous about a mating of convenience?" Rose asked. She eyed the bunch of them. "What if you met your fated mate afterward?"

Rose bit her lip. It was always a risk that one took, but it was rare that it happened. She tried to think of any stories she may have heard of this happening. Unfortunately, it would look like she would be one. Whoever the beta chose, eventually they would meet. Rose would be at the mating ceremony. It was her sister the woman was claiming. Her sister would be forever around and visiting. It wasn't like they would be able to avoid each other.

"The chances of that happening is low," Iris said. She shrugged and pushed off the bed to stand. "If we haven't met our fated mate by now, how would we? We've each traveled tons and have not stumbled upon that person."

"I agree. If that happens, then it would be something. I guess I would have to figure out what to do if that ever did happen," Harper said.

Rose sighed, not knowing what to do. She figured she would stay far away from the beta. Hopefully, it was just her bear wanting to claim someone powerful. What if the beta didn't feel what Rose did? What if it was all in Rose's head?

Her bear scoffed.

"It's time, ladies." Daisy glanced down at her watch. A devious glint appeared in her eyes. She was always up to something, and now that she was able to show off her skills, Rose was sure her sister's competitive nature was about to shine. "May the best woman win the heart of the beta."

Rose stepped to the side to allow her sisters to exit the room. She moved to follow them and paused in the doorway. Her heart was heavy watching them walk down the hall toward the festivities. She may try to ignore what her bear was telling her, but could her heart?

# CHAPTER FIVE

Mondo had spared no expense for this event. There was plenty of food, booze, and entertainment. Selen sat beside the alpha as his honored guest at a long table. The grand hall was filled to the brim with townspeople enjoying themselves. Tables were aplenty to allow people to dine while the center of the room was open to allow a direct path to the long table.

Beside Selen, Nick sat. The lead enforcer had been with their clan for years. The others were scattered throughout the room as an added layer of protection. Not that Selen felt threatened in any way, it was just that Nick was very proficient at what he did and he had orders from Eddie. The big enforcer didn't speak much while on duty. He constantly scanned the room. He ate very little and had pushed back his plate not too long after it had been brought to him. She smirked, knowing he'd be starving later.

Selen reached for her frothy mug of beer. The food that was served was top-notch. The cooks had certainly outdone themselves. She glanced down at her plate and looked at the mountainous pile of food that was still left.

A lone figure walked down the aisle toward them. Selen took a sip of her drink and eyed the enforcer for the Silver Fang. He was a bear of a man, as were most shifters. His hair was pulled up in a bun on top of his head. His eyes were fierce, and he even carried a large knife strapped to his waist. He paused before them and gave Mondo a nod. He turned his attention to Selen and repeated the same motion. It was a sign of respect. She recognized him as a leading member of Mondo's crew named Nathan.

Selen returned the gesture. The room fell quiet, and the music's volume dropped. The attention of everyone landed on him.

"Beta, the Silver Fang welcomes you and

your clan members tonight. We are honored to have you as an esteemed guest of our alpha and his mate." Nathan paused as the room exploded in applause and yells of support of their clan.

Selen sat up straight and swept the room with her gaze. The hairs on the back of her neck stood at attention. She wasn't sure why, but there was someone there watching her.

Sure, she was in a room full of people, but someone was gaining the attention of her bear. Her animal stood at attention, too. She breathed in deeply. She was greeted with plenty of different scents. The aroma of the food, cigars and cigarettes from a few townsmen, perfumes, that of every person in the room, but there was one scent that stood out from the rest.

It was sweet. Different. Her bear pushed forward, demanding she go and find that person.

Selen forced her bear back. Of course there were plenty of people in the room. Maybe it was just the slight nerves she was experiencing since she was here to claim a woman she had never met before.

The room finally settled down.

"It is I who am grateful for such a welcome for me and my men," Selen responded. She pushed back and stood. She raised her mug and turned slightly to Mondo.

The alpha and his wife, Goldie, were seated. She was a beautiful woman with long blonde hair. She resembled the painting that had been in Mondo's office. She was quiet and very welcoming to Selen.

"To the alpha and his mate for agreeing to such an alliance between clans. May this be the beginning of a long-lasting and close relationship between the Silver Fang and the Brown Claw."

Many cried out in agreement. She was met by applause and others in the room standing and raising their mugs and glasses. The townspeople of Chardon were very loyal to their alpha and Goldie.

Mondo and Goldie both grabbed their drinks and held them up for the toast. Selen took her seat and knocked back the rest of her beer. Luckily enough, with her being a shifter, it would take a lot for her to become inebriated. She slammed the mug back onto the table and offered the room a smile.

Everyone fell silent again to allow the enforcer to continue.

"Now for the presentation of the alpha's

daughters," Nathan called out. His voice echoed through the hall.

The nagging feeling of someone watching her was not going away. Selen scanned the room again and found plenty of people looking her way. The townspeople she was sure were curious about her. She brushed it off. Maybe the beer was affecting her mind and making her a little paranoid.

"You will have a hard time choosing one." Mondo elbowed Selen. He beamed like a proud poppa. He sat up straighter and motioned to the room.

First up was a tall, muscular woman with long blonde hair dressed in skin-tight black leather pants and a gray sleeveless tunic that put her arms on display. Selen could appreciate her powerful frame as she made her way down the aisle. She was beautiful and a mixture of Mondo and Goldie. The crowd cried out her name. She waved to the room and proudly came to stand next to the enforcer.

"May I present to you Daisy Bell. She is a member of our clan's enforcers. She is proficient in the use of many weapons, infiltration, and battle. She is known for her intelligence and strength," Nathan said. He motioned to Daisy and stepped aside.

Selen sat back and tried to appear calm. She kept her face devoid of any emotions. This was an important decision she would have to make. The woman she would choose would be by her side for all eternity. If she couldn't have the one who fate had designed for her and it was left up to her to make a decision, she didn't want to choose wrong.

Daisy grinned and lifted her arms. She showcased her thick muscles and spun around for the room to see. Selen bit back a chuckle. The woman may appear fierce, but Selen could instantly see the devilish look in her eyes. It reminded her of Mondo. She turned back to face their table with her gaze landing on Selen.

"Beta. I would make a fierce addition to your clan as your mate." Daisy confidently strode forward and stood before Selen. She didn't hide her perusal of her. There was a pleased air about her.

Selen tried to see if her bear was interested, but her beast chose that moment to be quiet.

"I look forward to chatting with you soon," Selen replied.

Daisy's grin spread wide. She gave a slight bow of her head. Selen would not be hasty in her choice. She wanted to speak with each of the women personally. She wanted to get to know them. She didn't have much time, but at least she wanted to have a conversation with them. See if they would even get along. That would be important to know.

"I can't wait." Daisy tossed a wink to Selen.

Mondo barked a hefty laugh at the antics of his daughter. It was apparent the woman was very competitive, even if it was against her own sisters.

Selen couldn't hold back the smirk. Her attention went back to the center of the room as another daughter came forward. This one was just as tall as Daisy but leaner. She wore a skin-tight black dress that stopped mid-thigh. Selen's gaze dropped down to the long span of her legs. They were toned and tanned. Her short blonde pixie hair stood up in spikes. Her nose was small, but it fit her face perfectly. Her lips were curled up into a cocky grin. Again, Mondo's and Goldie's genes were hard at work. The woman was a perfect mixture of the alpha couple.

"May I present Harper Bell. She is a world-renowned blacksmith. Her weaponry is sold near and far," Nathan boasted.

Selen perked up at the mention of the woman's profession. She was impressed that the figure before her crafted weapons. It wasn't that often she'd seen a woman in that line of work. Selen was impressed with Mondo's daughters thus far. It would seem they all possessed skills that could be useful. They were extremely stunning, intelligent, and had unique skills.

Mondo was right. It was going to be difficult to choose which daughter she would choose.

"It is an honor to meet you, Beta," Harper said. She strode forward to the table. She stopped before Selen. She reached under her dress.

Selen's eyebrows shot up at the sight of her pulling a small dagger from a sheath that was hidden on her thigh. Nick tensed up at the sight of the weapon. The bevel of the beautifully crafted dagger caught Selen's eye.

Harper expertly whipped it around and presented the handle to Selen. "A welcoming gift for you."

Selen took the dagger in her hand. The pearl handle was smooth. The steel shaft was perfectly made. Selen raised it to continue to assess it. She did love a good knife. She had a modest collection back home on the farm that she was proud of. She glanced back over to Harper.

"It is lovely. Thank you," she said.

Nick relaxed back in his chair. Harper nodded to her before sauntering over to stand beside her sister.

"Who said we were to offer gifts?" Daisy muttered.

But Selen heard her with her sensitive hearing. She bit back a chuckle the sight of the elder sister elbowing Harper.

"You should have known." Harper laughed. "I don't ever fight fair."

Selen grinned and placed the dagger down on the table. It would appear the sisters were competitive and taking this all in good stride. Selen had worried slightly that they may not want to be mated off for their clan, but it would appear they had no problems with it. Selen settled back in her chair as the final sibling began walking down the aisle.

This one was dressed in a loose-flowing, off-the-shoulder green dress. She was not as muscular as her sisters but had thick curves. Her skin was flawless, and her dark-blonde hair draped around her shoulders. Many eyes were glued to this beauty. Selen always did have a thing for soft, thick women.

She reached out to her bear again, but nothing. It would seem she was on her own. Her animal must be upset at her. The damn beast could be ornery and ignored Selen when she couldn't have her way. It was like dealing with a toddler at times.

"My name is Iris Bell," the woman said before Nathan could even open his mouth.

He scowled at the missed opportunity. Apparently, he took his job of presenting the women seriously. The young woman came to stand before Selen. A smile graced her lips. Her eyes were the same shade of the dress.

"I don't need someone to announce me. I can tell you all about me if you want to know."

Gorgeous and sassy. Selen couldn't help the smile that came forward. The woman was openly flirting with her.

"I plan to speak with each of you. I want to get to know all of you just a little before making any decisions," Selen said.

"Well, I'm sure Nathan was going to boast

about me, but I can tell you that I love to sing and am in love with the arts. Not only do I sing, but I love to paint and work with clay. I would be the best choice for you and your clan." She stepped back from the table.

Selen didn't miss the other two sisters rolling their eyes at Iris.

"I told you, Beta, this was going to be a hard choice." Mondo barked a hefty laugh.

Selen eyed the three women. They were all polished, powerful bears and would make wonderful matches. Anyone would be honored to have them by their side.

But who would be by her side? She had her work cut out deciding.

Selen leaned against the wall of the hall. The party was in full swing with music blaring, townspeople dancing, conversations loud and fierce. She had spoken with each of the Bell sisters and still had yet to decide which of the women she would choose. Her bear was indifferent to all of them, which left Selen frustrated and confused. Why wasn't her bear helping her? People accepted matings of convenience all the time.

Why was her animal being so damn difficult?

They each had qualities she should want in a mate. Daisy was strong and fierce and could help with the enforcers of Brown Claw. She had the experience and ideas that they could benefit from. Harper was spunky and had a sense of humor that rivaled Selen's. Her skills alone would benefit the town of Lurton, and Iris, her attractiveness and intelligence was something Selen had looked for in a woman. The youngest of the three was someone Selen could see herself having deep discussions with. She had a love for the townspeople, and someone like her would be an asset to Lurton.

"Have you made your choice yet?" Nick sidled up beside her. The enforcer had been her shadow the entire night. He folded his arms in front of his chest.

"Nope. How could I?" She smirked.

"I wouldn't want to be you right now." He snickered. His lips curled up in the corner as he glanced her way. "Three exquisite women to choose from? How will you choose?"

"I have no fucking clue." She snorted.

She eyed the table where the three women sat. They were enjoying the party, laughing at whatever they were discussing. Her gaze connected with Iris who gave her a little wave and a smile. Selen tipped her head in return.

She needed to think. Maybe fresh air was what she needed to help clear her thoughts so that she may decide on which woman she would claim. Mondo would want to know as soon as possible. Hell, she already knew she couldn't take forever deciding. That was why they'd had the presentation. To try and make it easier for her.

"Maybe spend the day with each of them. Try to get to know them a bit more than a short conversation at a party," Nick suggested. The bear's gaze scanned the room. Even though there were no threats, the enforcer never relaxed when it came to her safety.

"That would be idea," she murmured. It would mean she would have to spend more time in Chardon. She slid her hands into her pockets and tilted her head to the door. "I'm going to go outside and get some fresh air. I need to think."

She pushed off the wall and stalked away, not waiting for him to answer. He would follow her. She didn't have to look behind her to know. The other enforcers were spread out around the room. Mondo had been correct. No place was safer than this event. Not only were her men there, but Mondo had his enforcers there in full swing. She gave a nod to Abe as she passed.

She made her way through the beautiful lodge and exited through a back door. The immediate scents of the area accosted her. She jogged down the stairs and ambled down a path that took her away from the house. It was a stone pathway that went directly into the wooded area beyond it. The sound of the door closing behind her greeted her. She glanced over her shoulder and found Nick standing on the porch.

"I'm good. I need to be alone," she said.

He moved to protest, but she held up her hand.

"Seriously, I can handle myself, Nick. Give me some time and space."

"Yes, Beta," he replied.

He didn't look too happy but he would honor her request. She hadn't got into her position by being a weak bear. Her beast could handle herself if she ran into trouble.

"I won't be long. I promise," she added to try to soften her command. She turned back and continued along the path. The sound of the party grew fainter. As she went farther away from the lodge, she noticed little solar lights along the path giving a soft glow to the area.

It must be for the humans. Shifters had keen sight at night and wouldn't need the light. She did appreciate the beauty that it showcased. The trees were broad and went up high in the sky. Ahead stood a clearing with seating. It was cute, decorated with flowers and bushes.

Selen paused in front of the bench and glanced around. It did allow for someone to sit and enjoy the forest. The sounds of nature greeted her. Had she been in her bear form, it would be silent for the wild animals would sense a predator.

Selen took a seat on the bench and leaned back with her arm resting along the back of it. She inhaled sharply, the three women on her mind.

Her bear released a low growl.

A scent captured her and her animal's attention. Selen sat forward abruptly. Where did it come from? She glanced around and didn't see anyone along the path.

"What is that?"

It was delicious. Sweet. Alluring with a slight hint of musk. Her bear paced frantically. Selen didn't know what was going on. Now all of a sudden her bear was reacting to a mysterious smell.

When she'd met with each of the Bell sisters, she had scented them. Breathed in their unique aromas to test her bear. Her animal had remained indifferent to the women still.

But this was different.

It called to her and her animal.

Selen stood from her position. There was no one in sight, but that didn't mean there wasn't someone hiding off in the shadows.

"Is someone there?" Selen called out. She didn't want to scare the person. If they were hiding from her on purpose, then she didn't want to have them run off. She was a stranger in these parts and wasn't known. She took a step forward and swung around to eye the wooded area behind her. "I mean you no harm. Please. Don't go."

# CHAPTER SIX

Rose remained hidden behind one of the large trees. Her heart was pounding a mile a minute. Her bear paced frantically at the sight of the beta so close to them. Fear filled her. What if she presented herself and the beta didn't recognize her as her mate?

Rose's bear sure enough knew that this woman was hers.

But doubt slowly faded as Rose watched the woman scan her surroundings.

"I mean you no harm. Please. Don't go," the beta proclaimed.

Rose bit her lip and didn't know what to do.

Did she present herself and go over and say hello? She could. It would be rude to hide from her since she obviously sensed that Rose was in the vicinity.

Rose closed her eyes and leaned her forehead against the trunk of the wide tree. She had watched the presentation ceremony from the back of the room in a corner. It had pained her so to see how the beta had eyed her sisters. Daisy, Harper, and Iris would make someone a great mate someday. They were powerful, distinguished, and had the respect of their father. He was proud of the women they had become and was eager for one of them to be chosen by the beta to seal the agreement between the two clans.

"I give you my word. The word of the beta of the Brown Claw clan that I mean you no harm," the beta said.

Rose had learned her name was Selen Rawlyn. Even her name caused butterflies to appear in her stomach. She opened her eyes and pushed away from the tree. She held her head up high as her decisions was made.

She was a Bell, and even though she was not the chosen daughter of her father, she was still his daughter and she didn't hide from anything —or anyone. She would go over there, introduce herself to Selen, then she would promptly leave to give the woman privacy.

It was obvious she had a lot on her mind and needed to hash out whatever she was pondering.

*Like which sister she was going to choose to mate with.*

Rose grimaced and shook her head. She would be supportive of whichever sister was chosen. It would be expected of her. She dug down deep and found the strength to smile at her mate. She hoped that she could pull this off.

Introduce yourself.

Apologize for hiding.

Then leave.

It was simple enough.

Rose stepped around the tree and paused. Selen's keen gaze landed on her. The woman was dressed in a white button-down shirt with a royal-blue blazer. Her jeans were pressed with a deep crease in them. Her dark hair was left flowing along her shoulders.

But her eyes.

They studied her.

Watched her as she took a step forward.

Rose's knees trembled slightly. She inhaled sharply, and out of all the scents surrounding her from the woods, only one stood out to her.

Selen's.

Her bear slammed against her chest.

*Mate*, it screamed.

"Hello," Rose said. Her voice shook a little. She continued on until she was only a few feet away from the beta. She stepped onto the pathway and tried to remember her plan. Gazing into the beta's eyes had everything escaping. The only thing she could think of was how beautiful this woman in front of her was and how addicting her scent was. She inhaled again and wanted to memorize it. This may be the only time she would be close to this woman. She would need a reminder of what she was supposed to do.

Support whichever sister mated with Selen.

Not happening. The way her bear was reacting was just downright insane. Her bear was frantically clawing to get out. Her bear demanded that they switch positions so she could prove she was worthy to be the mate of a beta.

Rose stepped back.

"Hello there," Selen murmured. Her head

tilted to the side as she studied Rose. Her gaze slipped down Rose's full figure.

Rose's breath caught in her throat. It was as if she could feel Selen's hands sliding along her naked form. The skin along her arms prickled. Selen's eyes returned to her. The woman took a step forward to Rose.

Rose moved back a step. She couldn't allow the woman to get close to her. There was no telling what she would do. She had to fight to not race forward and bring Selen into her embrace.

"I didn't mean to hide. I didn't know who was coming. I was out here getting fresh air. I will leave you be," Rose stuttered over her words.

"My name is Selen. What is your name?" Selen asked. She took another step forward in an attempt to close the gap between them. Her nostrils flared, signaling she had caught Rose's scent. A heated glint passed through her eyes.

There was no denying it.

Being this close to Selen, there was no doubt in Rose's mind. This woman was her fated mate.

Shit.

What was she to do?

*Claim her*, her bear growled.

*No!* Rose replied to her animal.

"My name?" Rose tried to think of something clever to say instead of revealing it. But she drew a blank. She was not as quick-witted as Harper to reply with something snarky or even funny.

"Yes. I would like to know the name of the beautiful woman hiding in the woods when I arrived." Selen closed the gap between them.

Rose was frozen in place. Her mind was screaming for her to run away while her heart—and bear—demanded she stay.

Selen reached up and ghosted a finger down the side of Rose's cheek. "I could sense you the minute I sat down. Your scent. It called to me."

*Shit. Shit. Shit.*

"Maybe it was my perfume." Rose stumbled. She gave a shaky laugh and waved a hand in the air. She would need to distract her away from her natural scent. Damn shifters and their noses. "I just bought it and was trying it out for the first time."

"No, my dear. That is not the perfume I sensed. It is a lovely fragrance, but that is not what I was talking about, and I think you know that," the woman murmured. Her hand continued down to Rose's neck, then her shoulders, and slid down her arms. She captured Rose's hand in hers and brought it up to her lips. She pressed a kiss to Rose's inner wrist.

Rose had to lock her knees together because they threatened to give out on her. That would be embarrassing if she was literally brought to her knees by a beautiful woman paying her attention.

"My name...um...my name is Rose," she whispered. She was mesmerized by the woman. She inhaled deeply and welcomed the scent. She closed her eyes and savored the muskiness, the warmth of hidden sandalwood, and notes of a sweetness she couldn't put her nose on.

Was that honeysuckle?

Her bear rumbled in her chest.

"Rose. A pretty name for a beautiful woman," Selen murmured. Her lips ghosted Rose's wrist again.

"You shouldn't," Rose said. She tried to withdraw her hand from Selen's hold, but the beta held on to her tight.

"I shouldn't what?" She arched her perfectly sculpted eyebrow. Her thumb caressed Rose's sensitive skin. "What am I doing?"

"I don't know, but don't you have a mate to

choose?" Rose's animal didn't like that. She let loose a low growl. It poured out of Rose. Her eyes widened at the thought that she had just growled at an honored guest of her father. A beta, no less.

Selen chuckled and tightened her grip on Rose. She brought her flush against her and rested her other hand on Rose's waist.

"Now why does it seem you don't like that?"

"Um, it's none of my business. I'm sure my fath—" Rose cut off her words. She didn't want to let on that she was the other daughter of the alpha. The forgotten one. The one not allowed to be up for mating with a prime candidate who her father could use. "I'm sure the alpha would not appreciate you mingling with a random woman when you have been presented with his daughters."

"Mondo is not my alpha. I don't answer to him." Selen grinned.

Her lips were curled up into a sexy smile, and again Rose's knees grew weak. Thankfully, she was being held up by the woman's strong grip. She leaned forward and buried her face into the crook of Rose's neck.

The woman was boldly taking liberties. Rose

would otherwise shove someone else away, but she couldn't remove herself from Selen's hold if she wanted to. The feel of Selen's nose running along the column of her neck while she breathed in Rose's scent was so damn erotic. It brought carnal images of the two of them writhing in a large bed, naked together, to Rose's mind. She closed her eyes and whimpered. The image in her head was so damn real. Her body immediately grew flushed with the thought.

"No!" Rose exclaimed. She eased the beta back to remove her face from her neck. She shook her head and knew what the woman was doing.

Selen opened her eyes and stared down at Rose. Pushing her away was like trying to move a large bolder. She hadn't budged an inch. Her eyes narrowed on Rose. Something heated was in her eyes. Rose was unable to look away from her.

"What is your surname?" Selen asked.

"Please. I have to go," Rose whispered fiercely. Why couldn't she have followed along with the plan she had crafted before coming from behind that tree?

Introduce herself.

Apologize.

Leave.

All of that had gone out the window. Now here she was, caught in the woman's embrace, and she wasn't letting her go.

"Please…" Rose's voice trembled.

"What's gotten you so afraid?" Selen frowned.

Rose shook her head, refusing to answer that question. She didn't want to let on that she was afraid of her father finding out that she and Selen were mates. She wasn't a daughter who was considered worthy enough to present. He would certainly be angry with her if she ruined the agreement he had with the other clan.

Selen tightened her hold on Rose. Her hand on her waist moved slightly to her lower back. Rose wasn't going anywhere.

"Your scent. It is familiar to me. Tell me who you are."

"I told you. My name is Rose."

Rose reached between them again and pushed. This time the beta released her. She stepped away from Selen. A pain shot through her chest. It felt as if someone had taken a blade and stabbed her straight though her breaking heart.

"What is your last name?" Selen demanded again.

There was power in her voice, causing Rose's bear to want to submit to her. As the beta, she had power, and right now she wasn't fighting fair.

"I can't say," Rose whispered. Her eyes blurred from unshed tears forming. She blinked them away, not wanting them to fall. The last thing she wanted was her mate to remember her crying. She would stay far away from this woman. It was too dangerous. It was obvious Selen was picking up who Rose was to her.

And she couldn't allow that.

Selen was to mate with one of her sisters.

That brought more tears to her eyes, and she couldn't hold them back. She sniffed and took another step away from Selen. She moved to turn away, but Selen's hand shot out and gripped her wrist again.

"What do you mean you can't say? Who has you so scared? Tell me, and I will deal with them," Selen growled.

Rose blinked and allowed the tears to fall. It was a losing battle. She might as well tell her what she wanted to know. She would find out soon enough, and shifters had a second sense to detect lies. She reached up with her free hand and swiped at her cheeks. The wetness coated her hand. Rose held her head up proudly as she met the gaze of Selen.

"My name is Rose Bell."

The beta's eyes widened. Her hand fell away from Rose's wrist, freeing her. Rose spun on her heel and took off at a brisk pace down the path away from her father's home. The tears continued to fall. She didn't care. She allowed them to.

Her heart was breaking.

Her bear was growling, unbelieving that she was walking away from the one person who would complete them.

She was leaving her mate behind.

Rose wouldn't be able to support whichever sister mated with Selen. She wouldn't be able to attend the ceremony. She wouldn't be able to be around Selen at all.

She would go to her cabin in the woods and hide there forever if she must.

# CHAPTER SEVEN

Selen stalked toward the cabin in the foulest of moods. Had the alpha lied to her? Who was Rose Bell, and how was she related to the alpha? It was apparent the woman was scared. She had resisted sharing her true identity.

But Selen already knew.

The woman was definitely related to the alpha. Her scent was close to the Bell daughters'. But if she was one of his daughters, why wasn't she being offered up as a potential mate?

"Beta. Did something happen?" Nick appeared by her side and walked along with her.

She drew to a halt and faced him.

"I need to find out how many daughters the alpha has," Selen snapped. Her bear was pacing in her chest. There was no other reason her bear was acting the way she was.

Rose was her fated mate.

Her bear gave a growl, confirming it.

"What do you mean?" Nick asked.

She stepped closer to him and lowered her voice. "There was a woman in the woods. Her last name was Bell and—" She paused and eyed the building. She didn't know if anyone was listening to their conversation.

He leaned forward for her.

"I have reason to believe she is my mate," Selen finished.

He stepped back from her and jerked his head in a nod. He would find out the answer to confirm what she already knew in her gut. The reason Rose was terrified was that Mondo had to be her father.

"Yes, Beta. I will find out."

"I'm going to look over that damn contract again. I don't like the feeling I'm getting. He's hiding something," she said. She headed toward the cabin with the intent of going to the room she'd been assigned. She had a copy of the contract on her tablet.

"I will come to you with the answer shortly."

They entered the cabin and were met with another one of her enforcers who had been posted inside the door. Her team would never be far from her side.

"Where are the quarters they assigned me?" she asked Abe. She hadn't had the chance to go to it.

"The alpha is wanting to meet with you, Beta," Abe said.

She held up her hand and shook her head. She would not be meeting with him until she had pored over the contract again.

"Not now. I need my tablet," she said.

"Follow me." Abe didn't hesitate in guiding her through the home.

He took her down a series of hallways until they came to a grand staircase. The woodwork in this area was impeccable. There were large windows along the walls that allowed one to view the woods behind the house. Her gaze landed on the path that Rose had used to run away from her. Selen paused halfway to stare off at the landscape. Was her mate out there? Did she live somewhere in that direction?

"Beta?" Abe stood at the top of the stairs. His intense eyes were on her. "Is everything okay?"

"Yeah, it will be soon," she muttered. She pushed down her anger at the thought the alpha was trying to pull one over on her and her clan. Why would he hide a fourth daughter? Why would he instill fear into his own flesh and blood? She tore her eyes from the picturesque sight and continued up to the next level of the home. She followed behind Abe who brought her to a set of double doors.

"These are your quarters, Beta. Your belong- ings have been settled inside. We've already swept the area to ensure it is secured," Abe said. He moved to the side and stood with his back to the wall.

"Thank you. I am not to be disturbed unless it is Nick," she ordered. She opened the doors and stepped inside.

"Yes, ma'am."

She shut herself in and exhaled. She had to keep a balanced mind. She couldn't fly off at the hinges in a rage regarding her mate. As much as her bear wanted to break free and go after the alpha and demand to claim her mate, she had to be the levelheaded one of the two.

The room was immaculately decorated. It had neutral tones with the continued theme of the dark wood. The king-size bed was positioned on one side with a seating area. A door was open near the bed which she assumed was the bathroom. It gave a welcoming feeling, but at the moment she didn't feel too welcomed if the alpha had lied to her.

Her gaze landed on her leather messenger bag that rested on the small table in front of the sofa. She stalked across to it. She snagged her tablet out of it and slid her finger along the screen to awaken it. She pulled open the contract file and sat on the sofa.

The contract was pages long. She lost track of time as she skimmed the document. It was filled with so much legal jargon that any other day her head would hurt, but now she needed to find what she was looking for.

She had kicked off her shoes and rested her feet on the couch as she read. Her heart raced when she came to the section that discussed the offering from the Silver Fang as a good-faith gesture.

The daughters of Mondo and Goldie Bell.

She read through the passage, and it discussed how the alpha couple would offer the hand of their daughter for mating to the beta of the Brown Claw. The joining of the Bell family with the Rawlyn family would be a contract that could not be broken. The two families would allow the clans to become strong allies.

Selen froze.

She read through the section again.

It didn't mention the names of the daughters.

She read it again: the daughters of the alpha couple—that part was vague. Selen hadn't thought too much about it before. She had assumed the alpha would present all of his daughters. She tried to think of what she had heard of the alpha family before coming to Chardon, but she hadn't really paid attention to it.

She had researched him as an alpha and his dealings and if he were trustworthy.

But not how many children he had.

Selen bit her lip as she stared at the document. She moved through the rest of the contract and dropped down to the clauses and didn't see any mention of any daughters she couldn't mate with, only mentions of each clan remaining in control of their own people, no legal means to overthrow the other to control their clans, and how the clans would still remain their own separate entity.

A knock sounded at the door.

"Enter!" she called out.

The door flew open with Nick striding through it. She raised her eyebrows at him. She waved for him to come forward. He shut the door behind him and came toward her.

"Beta, I have news," he announced.

"Already?" she asked. That was quick. She would think that if the alpha had secrets that they would be well hidden and difficult to find.

"It wasn't hard at all. I asked several people in passing who worked here how many daughters the alpha had," he began.

The party appeared to still be in full swing. There were plenty of people in the lodge. Selen was sure something of this magnitude would continue on to the wee hours of the morning.

"And what did they say?" Selen blinked. This

was too easy. Just grab a random person in passing?

"They all confirmed the alpha and his mate had four daughters," he said. He stood to his full height and folded his hands behind his back.

She dropped the tablet to her lap so she could concentrate on what her enforcer was reporting. Her bear even paused her pacing to listen.

"The daughters of the alpha are Daisy, Harper, Iris, and Rose. Rose is the eldest of the children."

Selen stood abruptly. Her tablet fell to the floor, ignored. She scowled and moved away from the sofa. She paced with her mind racing. How dare the alpha lie to her. Why hadn't he presented all of his daughters to her?

Rose was beautiful. There was an intelligence in her eyes. Her scent.

Oh, goddess above, her scent. Selen closed her eyes and remembered the aroma she had breathed in when she had nuzzled the column of Rose's neck. She had ached to lick her, nip her delicate skin—sink her fangs into her and claim her.

"I was bold in my questioning and asked why

only three daughters were presented and was she maybe mated already."

Selen paused and spun around to face Nick. Had Rose already mated someone? A mating of convenience? Her bear slammed against her chest at the thought. The thought of someone else touching her mate, kissing her, tasting her— almost had Selen going into a blind rage. Her bear growled and pushed forward, demanding to be released.

"Beta, please. Control yourself," Nick suggested in a soft, easy manner.

Selen blinked and glanced down at her hands. Her claws had come out. She inhaled sharply, unable to remember the last time she had lost control of herself. She withdrew her claws and watched her hands morph back into her human form.

"I'm sorry," she muttered. She ran a trembling hand through her hair. She turned away and stalked over to a window. She rested her hands along the windowsill and stared out into the open view. Her room had a side view of the property. She could see the area of land where cars had parked. It was still filled to capacity. She guessed the people of Chardon really did like to party.

"Beta, is she your true mate?" Nick asked.

She closed her eyes and remembered the feel of Rose's soft skin. The feel of her wrist as she'd pressed a kiss to it. Her bear growled one word.

*Mate.*

She jerked her head in a nod. Rose Bell, the excluded daughter, was her fated mate.

"Is she mated?" Selen asked softly.

Was that why Rose had turned away with tears streaming down her face? Had she already committed to someone and knew they couldn't be together? That had to be the only answer. That had to be the only reason why Mondo would not include his other daughter in the presentation ceremony. He was known as a fierce alpha but fair. Would he deceive her and her clan?

"No, Beta. She is not mated."

Selen spun around to stare at her enforcer. Rose was unmated and yet was not included in the ceremony.

"What do you want to do?" he asked. He motioned to the door. "The alpha is asking to meet with you again. I'm certain he wants to know if you have chosen a daughter."

"I will not be meeting with him. Tell him I'm far into my cups or something. No decision will be made tonight." She spun back around and faced the window again. The sky was dark, sprinkled with twinkling stars. Was her mate out there, staring at the same stars she could see? The moon was high. It was only a half crescent. Was her mate staring at it?

Did Rose know they belonged together?

Oh, she most certainly knew.

"Yes, Beta. But—" The hesitation could be heard in his voice.

She already knew the question he wasn't asking. She stood to her full height and pushed down her animal. Her bear was strong-willed, but Selen was in control. Her bear would be irrational at the moment, and Selen had to keep a level head as she thought about what she was going to do.

"I need to find her. I want to speak with her. She will give me the answers I want to know. Apparently, this alpha likes to hide things, and I want to know why."

Selen had changed into comfortable clothing. She had thrown on a dark t-shirt and leggings. Official beta business was over. She was going to find her mate. If it had been so simple to find out how many daughters the alpha had, then she was sure she could find where Rose lived. It was obvious she didn't live in the alpha house.

"Are you sure you don't want anyone coming with you?" Abe asked. He walked alongside her as they made their way down the stairwell.

"I'm sure," Selen said. She was focused on finding her mate and getting some answers.

They exited the house through the same door she had left before. This time she wanted to question some of the townspeople, but would they tell her anything? She paused on the stairs and glanced over her shoulder at him.

"I'll be fine. I can protect myself. You men go enjoy what's left of the night."

Abe smirked. Nick wasn't going to allow that to happen, and Selen knew it.

"That's an order from your beta," she added. It wouldn't do them any harm to have a drink or two. They deserved it. They were hard workers and the best at what they did. "Tell Nick I said so."

Abe barked a laugh and headed back inside the lodge. Selen turned around and made her way down the stairs. Instead of walking the path, she followed the sounds of voices that were on the other side of the house. Laughter followed, signaling the females must have come from the party. Selen turned the corner and found two women walking toward the lot where the cars were parked.

"Where was Rose? Why didn't they include her? She's an upstanding citizen of our town," the taller of the two asked. She was young and had long dark hair and was dressed in jeans and an off-the-shoulder blouse.

"I'm not sure. Isn't it weird they never do? What did she do? She's beautiful, intelligent, and she's successful. She deserved to be presented," the short older woman said.

Luck was on Selen's side.

"Her apothecary shop is one of the most sought-after stores. I heard she has sales all over the country. So many people to go her with their ailments. Modern medicine doesn't have anything on Rose," the younger one said fiercely.

So her mate was intelligent and respected by her town. Everyone went to her for their ailments? She was a healer? Selen's curiosity was piqued even more.

She trailed behind them as they made their way through the lot looking for their car. Music was still blaring from the house. There were plenty of people in and outside of the home. Any other time, Selen would have appreciated how much the town of Chardon apparently loved to have a good time. Selen did as well, but at the moment she had a little more pressing matters to deal with.

"Excuse me, ladies," Selen called out.

She didn't want to startle the two. They hadn't even noticed that Selen had been walking behind them. They turned and recognized her. They shared a look then laughed.

"Beta, how are you? Are you lost?" the younger one asked.

She did a quick peruse of Selen. It was so swift that Selen almost missed it.

"No, I'm not lost. I couldn't help but overhear your conversation. Do you know where Rose lives?" she asked. She wasn't going to beat around the bush. She needed to get to Rose. Just listening to their conversation added to Selen's curiosity. There was a reason why Rose wasn't included, and it appeared even members of their own community weren't sure why.

"But of course we do," the older one replied. She suspiciously eyed Selen. The woman had a keen intellect that shone brightly in her eyes. She wasn't going to be easy to convince to give Selen information. "Why do you want to know?"

"I haven't been feeling well all of a sudden. I was told she would know what I should take to help settle my stomach and nerves," Selen lied smoothly. Well, not an all-the-way lie. Her nerves were shot right now, and she needed something to settle them.

Finding her mate would help.

"Oh, well, then if that's the case… Her shop is closed, but she does occasionally see clients at her home. She has an amazing garden where she keeps all of her herbs and sometimes makes her concoctions. I've taken my grandbabies there—"

"Mom, just answer her question. She doesn't

need to know your life story." The younger one rolled her eyes.

Her mother scowled at her before turning back to Selen.

"That's okay." Selen chuckled. She wanted to make sure they were at ease with her. Especially the mother. She had a right to be suspicious. A stranger asking for the home address of their alpha's daughter. Selen could respect that. She grimaced, reached up, and rested a hand on her stomach. She must have been convincing.

"She doesn't live too far from here. It's about a mile east. Take that path right there, and it will actually lead you directly to her home. The alpha had it made so that she could come home whenever she wanted to and have a clear path back to the house. Did you know that she moved out at the young age of eighteen? I swear that girl has been headstrong her entire life."

"Thank you, ma'am. I really appreciate it," Selen interjected. She didn't want to appear rude to them, but she truly didn't have time to listen to the woman ramble.

"Just tell her Cindy sent you," the younger one said. She gave a little wave and sent a wink to Selen.

"Of course. Thank you." Selen offered her a smile to Cindy and a nod to her mother.

She turned and headed in the direction of the small pathway. If Cindy's mother hadn't pointed it out, she would have missed it. The opening wasn't very large, just looked as if some trees were missing. It was dirt path that went deep into the woods.

She picked up her pace and began a slow jog. A mile wasn't too far away, but Selen was in a rush. There were answers she needed, and she wanted to hear them from her mate.

Her bear, realizing where they were going, stirred again. She pressed hard against Selen's chest, demanding to be let out. Of course, they could travel faster in their shifted form. Her bear was swift and could travel a mile in a much shorter time then her human legs.

"Not now. Later, I promise," Selen murmured. Soon she would allow her bear out. Hopefully, Rose's bear would come out so their animals could meet. Selen's bear seemed to be satisfied with the thought. She sat back and quieted down.

Selen needed to focus. When she arrived at

her mate's home, what would she say? Remembering the scent of her woman and the softness of her skin, Selen picked up her pace. She'd figure everything out when she got there.

# CHAPTER EIGHT

Rose stood in her kitchen and stared out into night. She raised her cup of tea to her lips and took a sip. She closed her eyes and savored the taste of her lemon balm tea. The zesty flavor was comforting to her. She raised the plant herself in her garden. It was great for stress relief. Tension filled Rose. Even her warm shower had done nothing to help calm her nerves or release the stiffness of her muscles.

Maybe she should move.

She would hate to leave the town she loved, but she had to put as much room as she could between her and Selen. Lurton wasn't that far away from Chardon. Maybe she needed to go to another state. They were in Montana. Maybe she could look for a clan in Maine, or Florida, or maybe even France. Clear across the world may put enough distance between them to cure her breaking heart.

Why did fate have to be so cruel?

She could deal with being in the strained relationship with her father and being treated less than her other sisters, but she really had put her trust in fate.

Her true mate was to be for her and only her. That person was to put her on a pedestal. Love her unconditionally. Treat her as if she were the most precious thing in the world.

Not having to pick one of her sisters to enter a mating of convenience.

Rose opened her eyes and sighed. What deity had she pissed off to render her so unlucky in life? She glanced down on her counter and saw a few of the latest flyers she had printed off for a sale she was going to have next week. She had brought them home to look them over.

Well, she at least had her shop. She always felt home there and she had poured her heart and soul into Rose's Apothecary. That would be her focus. She would push all thought of Selen from her mind. She would continue to grow her shop. She reached out and fingered the papers and knew that was what she would have to do.

That was her baby. It was what she had built with her own hands without the support of her family. She would continue to serve her community that she loved so much.

Another sip of her tea, and she started to feel her heart rate decline. She pushed away from the counter and left the kitchen. She had a good book to read that she had picked up at the local bookstore. She was always wanting to expand her knowledge of foraging for food and making natural medicines. She could admit she didn't know everything and wanted to better herself so she could help anyone who came into her shop.

She arrived in the living room. She had kept the decor cozy and homey. She sank down on her oversized couch and reached for the book that sat waiting for her on the coffee table. It was a large book and would take her a little while to get through it. She planned to make notes and study it.

With her thick blanket, tea, and a good book, she should be able to relax and maybe even grab some sleep. She had thrown on a comfy silky tank and short pajama set to ready herself for bed. She had been too wired to go straight to bed. So she decided to make her tea and read the book. That should make her sleepy enough. Rose chuckled and thought of how many times she had fallen asleep on her couch with a book in her lap. Tonight would probably be no different.

A knock sounded at the front door. Rose jumped and almost spilled her tea.

"Who the heck is that?" she murmured. She hastily took another sip before setting both the book and her mug down on the table. It was late, and the only reason someone would be visiting her cabin at this time of night was if they or someone close to them were ill. Her feet carried her to the front door swiftly. Her mind went to all of her medicines she had stored in her home and hoped she would have what was needed.

Rose arrived at the door and froze. It was beautifully crafted of wood with a half circle of a window revealing the back of the visitor. She didn't even have to turn around for Rose to know who it was.

Selen.

Even in the darkness outside, Rose recognized the outline and shape of her mate. She swallowed hard, her heart now racing again. Her bear sat up at the notion that their mate was at their home. Selen spun around, and their eyes met through the window. Rose reached over and flipped the switch to the porch light.

Maybe her eyes were deceiving her.

The light shone bright and highlighted Selen's beauty.

No. Her gifted shifter eyes were not failing her.

Rose's hand shook as she reached out and unlocked the door. She opened it slowly, unsure why Selen was there. Maybe one of her enforcers was ill and needed her assistance. She could handle that.

"Hello," Rose said. Her voice trembled slightly. She cleared her throat and stood to her full height. She tilted her head back so that she could continue to meet Selen's intense gaze.

"Rose," Selen murmured. They stood staring at each other for a moment before she motioned inside. "May I come in?"

"Why are you here?" Rose blurted out. She tightened her hold on the handle. She hadn't opened the door all the way. It was already unbelievable to think that her mate was standing on her porch. Now she wanted to come into Rose's home? This was her little hidden corner in the woods. She was already having to fight the bond that she knew existed between them. Having Selen here was going to cause her animal to go crazy.

"Why didn't you tell me who you were?" Selen replied. She stood firmly in place dressed in a dark shirt, leggings, and sandals. She didn't look like the powerful beta that she had projected earlier. Now she looked like a normal woman.

A woman who was slated to mate with one of her sisters.

"Because what does it matter?" Rose whispered. She shook her head and lowered her eyes. She was the daughter of a powerful alpha who thought less of her. Maybe something was wrong with her. She remembered watching her sisters be presented to Selen. Her father was right. What did she have that would be valuable to a potential mate? The fact that she liked to play in dirt and find plants, flowers, and fungi to make into homemade medicine? She wasn't as strong as Daisy, or had the talent of Harper, or was as beautiful as Iris.

She was just Rose.

"Let me in, Rose." Selen had yet to break the stare between them.

Rose snagged her bottom lip with her teeth as she thought long and hard. Did she let her in? Her fingers tightened on the handle, her mind racing.

Her brain—*no way, don't let her in.*

Her heart—*what are you waiting for? Let her in.*

"Please, Rose. We need to have a conversation in private. Not on the porch."

Rose blinked and nodded. She stepped back, allowing the door to open wide, and waved Selen in.

"Come in," Rose whispered.

Selen stepped across the threshold, and it was then Rose knew nothing would ever be the same again. Selen walked past her and paused while Rose closed and locked the door. She brushed by the beta and tried to not inhale her scent. It had already been teasing her when the woman had stood outside. Now that she was in Rose's home, it would take days for her scent to disappear.

"I...I was in the living room having some tea. Would you like some?" Rose asked and walked back into the living room. Having Selen here was sending her body into a frenzy. Her bear was pacing back and forth, her heart was pounding at an unnatural rate, while her libido was at an all-time high.

"No, I'm fine. Thank you."

Rose turned, and her core clenched at the sight of Selen standing in her home. She would have never thought this would ever have occurred. To keep her hands busy, Rose reached for her mug. If she didn't find something to do with them, she feared she would do something crazy like grab Selen and kiss her. Her eyes widened at the image that came to mind. She raised her drink and took a sip and prayed that the ingredients would once again calm her frazzled nerves. She motioned to the couch.

"Please have a seat." Rose moved over and sat in the recliner. There was no way she could sit next to Selen. It was already overwhelming that she was here, so sitting next to her would certainly be an issue. This woman was about to mate with one of her sisters. She didn't want to risk doing something that would ruin that.

Selen took her seat on the couch nearest Rose. Her gaze moved over to the book on the table. She lifted it and paged through it briefly.

"This any good?" Selen asked.

"I haven't read it yet. I just got it and planned to start it tonight," Rose murmured. She took another sip of her tea and wished she had made a bigger cup. She was almost done with what she had. She inhaled sharply and immediately regretted it. The aroma of Selen's natural scent filled her nostrils.

*Mate,* her bear growled. She slammed against Rose's chest, demanding to be let out. Rose fought to push her animal down. She needed to hear why Selen had come. If it wasn't to help someone who was ill, then why was she inquiring about who Rose truly was?

"I'm sure you don't want to hear about foraging and natural remedies. Why are you truly here?" Rose asked. She was never one to be straight and to the point, but at the moment she didn't have a choice. She needed to make this conversation quick so Selen could leave.

"Actually, I do. I want to know all about the daughter of the alpha who was not part of the presentation ceremony." Selen looked up from the book and settled her gaze on Rose. The beta was calm, but there was a weird glint that passed through her eyes.

Rose's hands trembled. This wasn't what she would want to share with Selen. It was little embarrassing to be known as the one daughter of the alpha who he didn't boast about. She was the disappointment to the Bell family. She lowered her gaze to the floor and shook her head.

"I don't know what to tell you. My father chose the three daughters he felt were worthy of being mated to a beta and presented them to you." Her voice was slight and barely considered a whisper. But she was sure Selen caught every word.

"What do you mean 'he chose?'"

The book slammed onto the table, and Rose jumped in her seat. Her eyes flew to Selen who leaned forward, resting her elbows on her knees.

"Why would he not be proud of all of his daughters? All four of you should have been at the ceremony."

"I was at the ceremony," Rose automatically replied. She clamped her mouth shut and dropped her gaze down to her mug. The tea was starting to cool, and she could finish it off in one, maybe two swallows. She sighed and wished she could have been a part of the presentation. But would Selen have chosen her? Did she feel what Rose felt? Was her bear going just as crazy as Rose's was at the moment?

"You know what I mean. Why were you not included?"

"I'm never included." Rose's eyes widened at the response that fell from her lips. She took a large gulp of her tea and swallowed it hard. She wiped her mouth with the back of her hand. "I've said too much. Please. Just go and pick one of my sisters—"

"Why?" Selen demanded.

Rose refused to meet her eyes now. This was getting to be more than she wanted to discuss. She didn't want to go into the fact that she was a disappointment to her father. That she never could measure up to her younger sisters. One would have thought that he would at least appreciate what his eldest daughter did for their community, but he did not. She wasn't a fully fledged healer. She only made the medicines that some of their most experienced healers from town needed.

She only went and found the rarest herbs and fungi that was needed to make concoctions that would be needed to heal and cure ailments.

No.

Her father didn't respect that.

"It nothing. Please." Rose's voice ended on a hiccup. She stood and motioned to the hall that led to the front door. "Allow me to escort you out."

"I'm not leaving until I get answers," Selen growled. She stalked over to Rose and snatched her mug from her hand. She placed it on the table and turned back to her. She cupped Rose's cheek in her warm hand.

Rose automatically leaned into it.

"Now tell me," Selen said. "Why does your father feel you are unworthy of mating with me?"

Rose's eyes flew to Selen. Her mouth dropped open in shock.

"I truly don't know." Rose blinked. Did she really know why her father didn't respect her as he did her siblings? No. She was just used to it. Sad to say, it had been this way ever since she was younger. "But my sisters—"

"It's not your sisters who I want," Selen cut her off.

Her grip on Rose tightened. Her head began to descend. Her eyes were burning bright with a fire that burned in them. Rose couldn't look away.

"It's you."

Selen's mouth crashed onto Rose's. Her body immediately responded with her mouth opening to greet Selen's tongue. She melted into her embrace. Her bear gave a victorious growl and urged her on. Rose's arms went up and wrapped around Selene's neck while the woman of her dreams kissed her.

She didn't know what to expect of this, but she was going to take what she could get. She would have to deal with the outcome in the morning.

# CHAPTER NINE

Selen's bear roared to life. The moment her lips touched Rose's she was a goner. Her woman's lips were as soft as they had appeared. From the moment Rose had opened her door, Selen's bear had calmed. She had paced frantically as Selen traveled on foot to Rose's home. Her cabin was deep in the woods and secluded away from everyone. Had it not been for the path that had been created, Selen wouldn't have found it immediately.

The walk had given Selen plenty of time to think. She had known there was something to Rose, and now that she was in front of her, she knew without a doubt that the other women were not for her.

This one before her, the one who's body was pressed against hers, was the one.

Fate, it would seem, had decided to show her face and present Selen with her true mate.

Selen's hand slipped up and dove into Rose's thick tresses. The silky strands held the faint scent of Rose's shampoo products which were ironically a rose aroma. She became lost in the taste of her mate. The taste of lemon had immediately greeted her the second her tongue had swept inside Rose's mouth.

Selen's bear grew frantic.

*Bite her*, the beast demanded. Selen ignored her animal. She couldn't—wouldn't—bite her immediately. They still needed to have another conversation, but right now, she couldn't tear her lips from Rose's if she tried.

Her grip on Rose's hair tightened as she deepened the kiss. She tilted her head to the side and felt her chest vibrate from her beast growling. Selen bit back a smile at her animal responding in kind.

Her hand moved up and pushed aside the skinny strap of Rose's top. Selen had reacted when she had taken in what Rose wore. She was obviously ready for bed. She was dressed in a soft pink silky tank-and-short combo, nothing else underneath it. Selen was able to see the shadow of Rose's nipples pressing against the thin material. It had taken everything she had to not reach for them the second she had walked into Rose's home.

Now, it was time for her to not only view them naked, but she needed to take those buds into her mouth. She glided both of the thin straps down Rose's shoulders. She showed great restraint in not ripping the top from her body. She tore her lips from Rose's and trailed them along the side of her face and down to the column of her neck. She inhaled the delicious scent of her arousal greeting her.

Rose's moan fueled Selen's desire. Her hands continued on their mission to rid Rose of her clothing. She drew the top down and snagged the shorts as well. They slid along her wide hips and dropped down to the floor.

Selen lifted her head then so she could take in the sight of her mate. What greeted her snatched all of the air from her lungs. Rose stood before her gloriously naked. Her large breasts were high and perky. Her areolas were wide and dark with her nipples drawn into little beads. Her stomach was flat but flared out into her wide hips. Her thighs were thick and absolutely perfect. Selen couldn't wait to feel their softness at the sides of her head.

Selen took a few moments to send her fingertips down the center of Rose's chest and down to her stomach. Her hands came to rest on Rose's waist.

"Where is your bedroom?" Selen asked. Her voice was low and husky. She couldn't stop touching her. Her bear was pleased that they had found the one who truly belonged to them. The damn animal wanted her to claim Rose immediately, but the human part of Selen knew she had to wait. There was still a formality she needed to follow, even though she was a beta and a strong bear.

"It's down that hall. Second door on the right." Rose hadn't taken her eyes off Selen. She tilted her head to the side toward the entrance to the hall.

Selen bent down and hefted Rose up by the backs of her thighs. She was pleased that she immediately wrapped her legs around her waist.

This position opened Rose to her and placed her core against Selen's stomach. She growled as the aroma of Rose's arousal grew thicker. Selen licked her lips and turned on her heel and headed toward the bedroom.

Rose dipped her head down and buried her face into the crook of Selen's neck. Her tongue slid along Selen's sensitive skin. A shiver passed through Selen at the feel of her mate nipping her flesh with her teeth. Another growl ripped out of Selen at the move. It was the move of her animal showing respect to Selen's.

She burst through the door and found the room to be cozy with a large bed at the center. She zeroed in to the bed and stalked toward it. She paused in front of it, still holding Rose in her arms. She kicked off her sandals just as Rose lifted her head and pressed her lips to Selen's.

Their kiss was deep and full of passion. Selen leaned down and gently deposited her onto the bed. Her arms were still entwined behind Selen's neck. She fell forward onto her mate. They rolled onto the bed, a tangled mess of arms and legs. Selen positioned herself to where she landed on top.

It was time for her to take a taste of her mate.

"Selen," Rose groaned.

Selen scattered soft kisses to her lips before she moved farther down. She massaged and gripped Rose's mounds in her hands. The woman's breasts were exquisite and large. They spilled out over Selen's palms. She lowered her head and captured one of the dark buds with her lips. She suckled it into her mouth, and her core clenched. Her pussy was slick with need, but at the moment, the only thought she had was to taste every inch of her new lover. She would push her needs down.

There was no reason Rose should ever feel unwanted. Selen didn't know what the alpha's problem was, but now that she was here, Rose would never experience the feeling of being unwanted or less than. This woman was the perfect specimen for Selen. Fate knew it, and that was all that mattered. Selen would deal with the alpha. She would not claim either of the women who had been presented.

Rose was hers.

Her mate's body arched from the mattress as Selen released the first soft bud and swiped her tongue across her chest to the other one. She brought that nipple into her mouth and bathed it with the tongue. The hard bud was a soft pebble. She played with it, teased her, drew it farther into her mouth.

"Yes," Rose moaned.

Her fingers dove into Selen's hair and held on to it. Selen welcomed the tugging of her strands. The pain was slight, but she loved it. She released the nipple she had been suckling and sent her tongue over the entire mound. Her mate's breasts were so damn delicious that she could stay here for hours suckling them.

But there was somewhere else she was needed.

Her tongue went on a journey. She wanted to taste every inch of Rose and learn all there was to know about her. Being a bear shifter, her tongue was more enhanced than a human's. It was a benefit of being a shifter. Her mate's soft skin trembled, and she made her way to her stomach. She dipped her tongue into Rose's navel which caused a giggle to escape her lips. Selen loved the sound and knew she was going to do her damnedest to ensure she always had a reason to laugh and smile. She wasn't sure what

Rose had to endure growing up under the thumb of Mondo, but Selen was here now and she would take care of her.

She reached down and raised her legs, arriving at her core. The aroma of Rose's arousal sent her bear into a mating frenzy. She had to push her animal down to keep her from pressing forward. Selen's hands shook as she took her first glance at her center.

She was perfect.

There was a small patch of hair that was kept neatly cropped low. The brown curls were the same color as Rose's hair. Her labia were plump, and the sight of her swollen clit captured Selen's attention.

Her mate's little pearl was seeking her.

"You are true perfection," Selen murmured.

She dragged her finger along Rose's fat lips and dipped it between them. She was met with slick honey. Selen's chest rumbled a pleased growl at the sight of her creamy white liquid coating the finger. She lifted it and licked it clean. The taste that exploded on her tongue had another growl erupting from her. She spread Rose wide to reveal her entire pussy for her. She dipped her head down and sent her tongue on the same path her finger had just traveled. She gathered the creamy goodness on her tongue and was lost. It was a taste that was only her mate and one that she would never tire of.

Rose was sweet, just as Selen knew she would be. Her tongue glided down the complete length of Rose's pussy before traveling back up to her clit. Her lips closed around it and sent Rose's body arching off the mattress again. Selen used her free hand to press her back down onto the bed. Rose's gasps and moans filled the air. The sound of her pleasure was fueling the fire that was blazing inside Selene.

She played with Rose's swollen bud, suckling it deep into her mouth before bringing her tongue into action. Her hands rested on Rose's thighs, keeping them open for Selen to consume all of her.

She devoured her mate, more of her slickness dripping out of her cunt. Selen ensured that none of it went to waste. She was in total control of her mate and her pleasure. She wanted Rose to feel desired, to feel love, and to have extreme pleasure like she had never known before.

After tonight, Rose would never feel unwanted ever again.

"Oh!" Rose exclaimed.

Selen's tongue flicked along her bud while she pushed two fingers deep inside her. Selen's fingers were coated with arousal. The creamy liquid completely drenched Selen's fingers and her hand. Rose was not quiet at all when it came to her pleasure. Her moans grew louder, and her hips undulated from the mattress. She rotated them around. Selen fucked her mate with her fingers while she continued to focus on her swollen bud.

Her chest swelled with pride to know that she was giving pleasure to her. A bear was very possessive of their mate and wanted to be the only one to please, provide, and protect them. And all of this, Selen would do.

"Yes, keep going," Rose called out.

Her gasps and demands were sending an electrical current through Selen's body to her pussy. Her panties and leggings were sure to be soaked. She could feel her own juices pour out of her, and she consumed her mate.

She added another finger inside Rose, stretching out her taut muscles. She thrust them in hard and in a steady rhythm. Rose's hips gyrated and met each of her thrusts. Her grip on

Selen's hair tightened to an almost unbearable pain, but Selen welcomed it. She didn't care if Rose ripped her hair out at the roots. She would proudly rock the bald patches as a symbol of pleasing her.

Rose's body shook, but Selen continued. Rose kept her legs raised to allow Selen to have full access to her pussy. Selen reached up with her free hand and fondled one of Rose's breasts. She took the mound in her hand and teased her nipple.

"Selen!" Rose chanted her name and rode her face.

Her mate was not being shy at all. She had appeared shy in the woods earlier that day and even when Selen had first showed up at her home. Selen wasn't sure if Rose would have let her in. She had certainly hesitated when she'd first answered the door.

But now that Rose was spread out on her bed before her, the true nature of her was showing, and Selen loved it.

Selen squeezed and tugged on Rose's nipples while she flicked her clit with her tongue. Rose's body stiffened. Her inner walls clamped down on Selen's fingers, and she crested. Her head flew back, a scream erupting from her. Selen watched with bated breath. Her mate held on to her own legs and rode the waves of her orgasm. Her release gushed from her, drenching Selen's face and shirt.

Selen ignored it and wedged her fingers in as far as she could while she latched on to Rose's clitoris. She didn't let up on it and suckled it as hard as she could. Rose's body shook the bed as she trembled. Her voice grew hoarse, and she chanted Selen's name once again. Her body flopped back onto the bed. Her muscles relaxed while she lay there. Her legs slowly came down. Her feet perched on the bed.

Selen grinned and released Rose's clit. She eyed her woman who lay sprawled on the bed with her eyes closed. Her chest was rising and falling swiftly. Selen zeroed in on the sound of Rose's heart racing. She spread her legs wide again and licked her. There was so much of her sweet honey that had released from her, that Selen needed to clean her. None of it would be wasted. So she took her time and licked every inch of Rose's pussy to ensure she had consumed it all.

Once she was satisfied she had cleaned her as

well as she could, she got up off the bed. She tugged her shirt over her head and tossed it onto the floor. She quickly removed the rest of her clothing. Just as she thought, her panties and leggings were drenched from her wetness that poured out of her.

Selen eyed Rose who was beautiful in her post-climax state. She crawled alongside her on the bed and kneeled by her head. Rose's eyes snapped open and connected with Selen's. Her heated gaze slid along Selen's naked frame. She licked her lips and reached for Selen.

"I need your pussy on my tongue," Rose said.

"Of course you do." Selen smirked. Her mate was all bear. Sensual, vocal when it came to lovemaking, and needy. Selen would give her mate everything she ever asked for.

She tossed her leg over Rose's head so she straddled her face. Rose's hands came to rest on Selen's thighs. Selen lowered her aching pussy down to Rose's waiting mouth. The second it covered her, Selen released a growl. She glanced down and took in the sexy picture her mate made, welcoming Selen sitting on her face.

Selen gave off a possessive growl at the sight. Rose was absolutely beautiful, and now she had her face between her legs. Selen reached down and threaded her finger in Rose's hair.

Yes, she would give her exactly what she needed and wanted. In the morning, they would discuss their plans. Selen was not leaving Chardon without her. She was ready to put up a fight.

The only person who would be by her side when she left would be Rose.

Selen threw her head back and basked in the feeling of her tugging on her clit. A moan slipped from her. She would enjoy her for the night, but come morning, she would be having a conversation with the alpha.

# CHAPTER TEN

Rose snuggled down into her bed. She didn't want to open her eyes because then she knew reality would reveal itself. She knew exactly what she had done last night and well into the morning. Again, she would be a disappointment to her father. She had slept with her mate—the woman who should be choosing one of her sisters.

But how would she deal with this now? She'd had a taste of Selen. She licked her lips and could still taste her on her tongue. Selen's cunt was so damn delicious, she was already addicted to it. Even the thought of someone else licking her had her bear awakening.

They would not stand for that. A possessiveness like she'd never known before reared itself inside her.

Rose's eyes snapped open. She tried to will her racing heart down, but it was too late. Her bear was already in a state of rage at the thought that once Selen left them, she would be going to Rose's father to choose one of the other Bell sisters.

Rose's gaze landed on Selen's hand that was cradling her breast. Her lover had awakened something inside Rose that she was unfamiliar with. Selen's bear had connected with hers. Even though they had remained in their human form the entire night, their bears had heard each other. Through their growls and roars during their lovemaking, the two bears recognized each other.

Rose's vision blurred suddenly. Tears came forth that she didn't need. She wouldn't give in and cry. When Selen left, *then* she would allow herself to cry, but until then she would appear to be strong. Rose had decided to be selfish for once in her life and take what she wanted and needed from Selen.

It was a good thing that neither of them had bitten each other. Rose's gums were swollen and tender. Her fangs had wanted to descend. She had fought them and kept them away. Had they come out, she was sure her beast would have taken over and bitten Selen. The urge had been there all night.

*Claim her,* her bear whispered. Rose shook her head and lifted it from the crook of Selen's arm. The sleep she'd had was the best she had gotten in a while. Being in the cradle of her mate's arms was where she wanted to remain. Selen's toned body was warm and enticing. Rose had kissed and licked every square inch of it. She wanted to memorize every part of her.

She may never have this chance again.

Her gaze roamed Selen's naked body, and a stirring set up home between her legs. Her core grew wet at the sight of Selen's firm, high breasts. How Rose wanted to turn and snuggle down and suckle her. That how she imagined waking up in the morning. Turning over and taking her nipple in her mouth. Or sliding back down and diving between her legs again. The tanginess of her arousal still lingered on her tongue. She would love nothing other than sliding her tongue between her mate's slick labia.

But no. This woman couldn't be hers. Even though fate had determined it, a binding contract was going to say otherwise.

Rose's bear slammed against her chest in a rage. Rose's eyes widened at the sight of her dark fur spreading along her arms. She tried to rein her animal in, but her bear wasn't listening to her. She pushed off the bed and stumbled onto the floor.

*No*! she yelled at her animal.

*Mate*! her animal growled. She slammed against Rose's chest again, demanding to be set free. Never in all of her thirty-three years had she lost control of her animal.

"Rose? What is it?" Selen's sleep-filled voice sounded behind her.

Not wanting her animal to break free while in her house and tear stuff up, Rose pushed up off the floor and headed out of her room. She fell against the wall of the hall. Her animal pressed forward more. The change was coming, and she was unable to prevent it. She raced through her small cabin and headed into the kitchen toward her back door. She slid it open just in time; her talons broke free. She fell down the stairs and onto the thick grass, and her body began to morph into her bear.

The faint sound of Selen calling her name met her, but her bear was taking over. Rose cried out and tried to resist, but her animal was overpowering her. More of her fur sprouted from her skin, her bones beginning the transformation. They lengthened, grew thicker as her bear emerged.

Soon her animal was free. Rose stood on her hind legs and threw her head back and roared.

She was in shock that her bear had overpowered her. Why would her animal defy her? Was she weaker than her animal? Her father would certainly—

"Rose!" a sharp voice cut through her racing thoughts.

She turned and fell down on all fours. Selen came out of the house slowly. Her eyes narrowed on Rose. She came to the edge of the porch. She hadn't put on any clothing, and in the daylight she was pure perfection.

Rose's bear gave a low growl. Her eyes

widened at the defiance of her bear. Selen ignored her bear's growl and came down the stairs. She walked toward Rose, and it was then she was hit with the waves of her mate's power. Even in human form, her bear was strong and showing that she was in control.

Rose tried to fight and gain control of her unruly bear, but her animal wasn't listening.

"You are a beautiful animal," Selen murmured. She came over to Rose and ran a hand over her bear's head.

Her animal folded, no longer filled with rage. Was all she wanted to do was show herself to Selen? Her animal practically purred and pushed her large head into Selen's chest.

"You wanted me to see you, didn't you?"

Her bear gave off a snort. Rose rolled her eyes at the way her bear was acting. She had demanded to be let out, forced her way out, and now she was preening in front of Selen. Rose sat back in awe at the feelings that were rushing through her. Her bear didn't want them to lose out on their mate.

She wanted to come forward and reveal herself to Selen.

The bear was more stubborn than Rose, apparently.

"I already sensed you, my love," Selen murmured.

She scratched behind Rose's ears, and even Rose had to close her eyes and enjoy the feeling. Her mate was comforting her bear. Her animal was the average size of a female bear. She weighed in around six hundred pounds and was bulky. Another purr escaped Rose's animal.

"Are you here to make your argument for us?"

Rose stepped back from Selen. Her bear gave off another growl, agreeing with Selen.

"Well, since you are here, why don't you meet my animal. She is here and wants to come forward." Selen stepped back, and immediately her body began to go through the change. Her dark fur sprouted forward, and she fell to the ground. Her body contorted and reshaped into her animal. Soon a magnificent bear stood before them. Her grizzly was beautiful and large. Rose gave an appreciative growl at the size of her. She stepped forward and immediately nuzzled her face into the neck of Selen's beast.

It was a show of submission to the stronger

animal. Rose rested back and allowed her bear to lead. Now that she was there and her mate's animal was present, they might as well allow the bears to get acquainted.

But what would happen when it was time for Selen to leave?

*Mate*, her bear snapped. Rose grew worried about how her animal would react, but then a sense of possessiveness came over her.

Why couldn't she mate with Selen?

This was her fated mate. No man or shifter should stand between what fate had aligned for them. This was bigger than a contract. If her father tried to stop them, would fate intervene?

Rose pulled back and stared into Selen's dark eyes. She licked Rose's nostril and motioned with her head for them to go into the woods. Rose followed Selen and knew that this was going to be the beginning of their mating.

She would fight for her.

She would no longer stand aside and allow her father to make decisions for her. Even if she had to confront him, she would. She was not going to allow Selen to go off and form an alliance with another woman.

Selen was hers, and Rose was going to do

what she had to do to ensure that they would be together.

*Finally,* her bear snorted.

Rose's mouth dropped open at the sassiness of her animal, but then she had a sense of warmth and support wash over her. Rose's bear was giving her the sign that she would back her up. Never did she have any doubt that her bear wouldn't. They were the same person and shared a body. It may have taken the human side of her to come to this conclusion, but she was glad that her bear was on the same page.

They would claim their mate.

Damn what her father thought.

She followed Selen, and they spent hours in the woods just traipsing along and allowing their bears to get to know each other. They played together, found a stream and caught a few fish together, and snacked. It was a day that Rose would never forget. It was the day that she would admit that she fell in love with Selen. Something as simple as being together, alone in the woods, was freeing to her.

The sun was high. They lounged on the bank of the stream in the soft grass. Rose looked over at Selen's bear, and it was then she decided she needed to come forward. She and Selen needed to speak. Not as animals, but in their human form. She had so much to say that she needed to get this off her chest now while everything was fresh in her mind.

*I need to speak with her. Give me control,* Rose demanded of her animal.

Her bear thought about it for a moment before giving a nod.

Well, that wasn't hard.

Rose pushed forward, and the change began. Her larger body shrank, and the fur that coated her dissipated. Within moments, she was back to her human form. Selen raised her head from where it rested on the ground.

"Hey there," Rose murmured.

She gave a wave to Selen's animal. She crawled over to her and rested a hand on Selen's snout. She pushed her nose into Rose's palm. A sense of calmness came over Rose. Her bear was helping her.

She smiled and gave Selen's nose a little rub. "I need to speak with Selen. Can she come forward?"

Selen's bear tilted its head to the side as she studied her. Rose bit her lip and waited patiently.

"Please. I really need her," Rose said softly.

The air around Selen shimmered, and she transitioned back into her human form. Her power allowed her change to happen much faster than Rose's. They stared at each other for a moment before Rose flew forward toward her. Selen caught her, and they fell back on the thick bed of grass. Her warm arms wrapped around Rose.

She sniffed and buried her face in the crook of Selen's neck, racked with emotions. This woman was hers, and she was in love with her. She held on to her tight and didn't want to let go.

"What is it, my love?" Selen murmured.

Her lips brushed the top of Rose's head. Their naked bodies lay entwined together. The warmth of the sun kissed Rose's skin, and she had a true sense of what heaven must be like. She didn't ever want to move from this spot. If she and Selen could stay here forever, she would be one happy bear.

"So you felt it, too?" Rose's lips breezed over Selen's skin.

It took all of Rose's willpower to keep her fangs from dropping through where she could mark Selen. Even though she was sure Selen wouldn't be here with her if she didn't, Rose needed to hear her stay the words.

"Didn't you hear me when I said that it's you I want?" Selen tugged on her hair to force Rose to meet her gaze. Her eyes were a dark shade of brown, almost black. Her fangs peeped through underneath her lips. "You are mine. No other will do for me."

Selen leaned down and pressed a chaste kiss to Rose's lips.

"You are the one for me, too," Rose whispered.

Selen's leg was braced between Rose's thighs. Rose felt like a wanton hussy; she ground down on Selen's leg. The need for her was rising again. Selen's soft growl reached her ears. Her grip on Rose's hair tightened.

"It would seem my mate is in need of my tongue," Selen said.

Her hand slipped between then and parted Rose's folds. Another growl, this time much stronger, escaped from her lips, and she was met with the proof of Rose's desire for her. Rose groaned and thrust her hips forward, Selen's finger encircling her aching bud.

"Yes. I need you." Rose leaned forward and nipped Selen's chin. The act caused her gums to swell and ache, her large fangs dropping down.

She would not place her mating mark.

Rose repeated this over and over in her head. Not until they could officially mate. They first had to go to her father.

Selen boldly strummed her clit. Rose threw her head back and moaned loudly. She didn't care who may be nearby and hear them. Selen rolled them over where she was braced over Rose. Her finger felt so damn good, but Rose couldn't wait for Selen's tongue to find its way to her pussy.

Rose spread her legs wide and offered herself to her. She didn't care what she looked like. She was in desperate need to have her mate devour her and send her off to the stars.

"Look at you opening yourself for me." Selen chuckled. She dropped a hard kiss onto Rose's lips. She pushed up and slid down Rose's body. "Hold these legs out of the way, my love. I want all of you."

"You can have all of me." Rose didn't hesitate to comply. She lifted her legs and kept them spread open for her. Her core clenched, and

Selen dove between her thighs and feasted on her.

Rose's breath caught in her throat. She stared down at Selen's dark hair between her legs. She reached out and entwined her fingers in the strands so she could hold on for the ride.

# CHAPTER ELEVEN

Selen stalked through the halls of the alpha's lodge. It had taken everything she had to leave her mate. Rose's wide eyes still haunted her. She had insisted in coming with Selen to confront Mondo, but this was something that Selen would need to do on her own. She was a beta and she was a strong bear. This alpha was going to have to explain why he had been untruthful about the daughters he had.

"Beta, is everything okay?" Nick arrived at her side.

She should have known he would be keeping

an eye out for her. She had been gone less than twenty-four hours away from the cabin.

"It will be," she replied. Her bear was in a mood. She hadn't wanted to leave their mate either. After the time they had spent together, it was without a doubt that Rose was theirs. Selen had half a mind to claim Rose down by the stream, but she wanted to wait. She wanted their mating to start off on the right foot. She wanted to ensure Rose knew how much she meant to her.

Even if she had to create an enemy in Mondo, she would. Eddie would back her up. Her alpha would have her back one hundred percent with no explanations.

"The alpha has been demanding that you come and meet with him," Nick announced.

"I'm sure he has," she muttered.

They reached the stairs that would take her up to her quarters. The house was much quieter than when she'd left. The party must have officially ended. The only people she saw were those on the cleaning crew working diligently to restore the house after the event.

Selen took the stairs two at a time with Nick following her upstairs.

"How do you want me to respond?" he asked once they arrived at the second level of the home.

They made their way to her suite and paused in front of the door. She turned to him and thought about how she should respond. Did she let on that she had found her fated mate and would not be honoring the contract?

"Should I tell him that you have found your mate?" he asked.

She arched an eyebrow at the enforcer. His lips turned up in the corner in a small smile. Selen narrowed her gaze on him.

"I can smell your mate on you." He cleared his throat, the smile disappearing.

"Considering the relationship of my mate to the alpha, we are going to go through with the contract. Only he's going to include my mate as she should have been from the beginning," Selen stated. She would go and clean herself up, then she would meet with the alpha, but it would be on her own time. She didn't care if he had to wait. She opened the door and paused to glance over at Nick. "Tell him I will meet with him in one hour."

"Yes, Beta." He bowed his head to her and spun on his heel and stalked away.

She closed the door and entered her private domain. She glanced around and found the room to be in the same state it had been in when she'd left. She inhaled and didn't pick up on the scent of anyone being in her room while she was gone.

Selen went over to the nightstand by the bed and picked up her phone. There was a missed message from Eddie.

*Everything going as planned?*

Selen stared at the message before she responded.

*There is a slight deviation, but we shall see how it plays out.*

She placed her phone back down and went into the bathroom. She stripped off her clothing and tossed it to the floor. She didn't want to wash her mate's scent off her, but she must. Showing up to a meeting smelling of his daughter would be a bit much.

Selen started the shower and went over and relieved her bladder quickly while the water heated up. She was just in disbelief that Mondo would feel that Rose would not be worthy to be mated. Her mate had much to offer. They'd had a long conversation after their spirited love-making session by the stream. On their way back to Rose's cabin, she'd shared with Selen her work on foraging and making homemade medicinal remedies. Selen was in awe of her. During their walk, she'd pointed out herbs that Selen would have assumed were weeds or worthless flowers.

She had been blown away by her mate's knowledge of the forest and what was inhabited there. How could Mondo not see the value in what Rose did? Her shop was located in town, and according to Rose, she had used the money she had saved to open it.

Selen finished her business then went over to the shower. The temperature was warm, and steam had clouded the air. She stepped into the shower, and pride filled her at Rose's accom-plishment.

Selen had one intention when she entered this meeting.

Claim her woman.

Mondo would have no choice but to allow her to claim Rose. Not only was she Selen's choice of his daughters, but she was Selen's fated mate. If he were to try to stop her, then Selen would not hesitate to defy him and take Rose with her. She didn't care that the contract would be voided.

This was her woman, and she was not going to let anything stop her from claiming her. Selen was only being kind even going to him. She could have just claimed Rose and dealt with the outcome, but that wasn't her style. She had honor and a code. Her clan depended on her to keep a levelheaded approach when dealing with other clans.

But if he stood in her way, then he would gain a new enemy in her.

Her chest rumbled; her bear agreed with her.

Selen quickly washed her body and her hair. She hated that the scent of Rose would no longer be as strong as it was. If she closed her eyes she could still taste her cunt, hear her cries of ecstasy, and feel her powerful legs clamp down on the sides of her head.

Selen smiled. It would be only a matter of time until Rose would be hers. They would have to talk about the shop and how they would manage it. She smiled thinking of Rose coming out to her farm. She would be encouraged to plant whatever she desired on her land. Selen had plenty of acres that would welcome the attention of her mate.

"**B**eta, the alpha awaits your company in the study," one of Mondo's enforcers greeted her at the bottom of the staircase.

She had seen him before but was unable to remember his name. Nick and Abe stood behind him. She was unsure what was going on, but she was sure they would update her as soon as possible.

"Lead the way," she replied dryly.

She didn't like being met and escorted to the alpha. She followed behind the enforcer. She raised an eyebrow at Nick as she walked past him. He gave a short shake of his head, and she relaxed. If there was an issue, he would have interrupted her in her room to notify her. Her men followed directly behind her as they were led to the room where Mondo was waiting for her.

Mondo's man reached for the door handle and opened it for her. He waved her inside.

"Thank you," she murmured.

The hairs on the back of her neck stood on end. She immediately erased all emotions from her face. The study was a large room filled with shelves of books that spanned each of the walls. A roaring fire was burning bright in the fireplace with two oversized high-backed chairs placed near it. Mondo stood before the fire with a glass in his hand and stared into the flames. He made a striking figure with his unruly dark hair, broad shoulders, and muscular physique. He eluded power, and his alpha waves were gently filling the air.

Selen scanned the room and saw Nathan, Mondo's lead enforcer, standing off in the corner. She motioned for Nick to join her. Abe would remain outside to guard the door. If Mondo had a man inside, so would she.

"There is something about the power of fire that is so captivating, wouldn't you say, Beta?" Mondo said.

He lifted his glass and took a sip out of it. He turned slightly and eyed her as she approached. She held her head high and met his gaze head-on. He may be an alpha, but she was no weak bear. He could try to intimidate her, but he would fail.

She came to stand a few feet from him near the fire. She tilted her head and took him in. There was a strong resemblance between he and Rose. She just did not understand how he would think so little of his firstborn.

"Have the kind of passion that sets the world on fire," she replied. It was a quote she had heard years ago that had stuck with her. It was something that she had yearned for. The love of her mate would fuel the passion inside her that could set the entire world on fire.

With Rose, that was how she felt.

"A poet, are we?" He arched an eyebrow at her.

She shook her head and glanced down at the fire. "Not hardly. Dalai Lama said those words. I read them in a book years ago, and they have always stayed with me," she said. The flames were high, and the heat that radiated from the hearth was warm and welcoming.

"Have a drink. We have much to discuss," Mondo urged. He motioned over to the table near the hearth that held a small decanter and glasses.

"I'm good." She shook her head. She needed to keep a clear mind for the conversation they were about to have.

"Well then. Have a seat. I am anxious to hear if you have made a decision. I'm sure you are ready to go back to Lurton," Mondo said.

They took their seats in the chairs that faced each other. Selen relaxed back and crossed her jean-clad legs. She had chosen to remain slightly casual for this meeting. She had on a pair of jeans with a light-colored blouse.

"Anxious to get back home, that I am," she admitted. But she glanced around before landing her gaze back on him.

He barked a hefty laugh.

"Not that I don't appreciate your hospitality," she said, "but home is home."

"Well, let's just cut to the chase," he said. He knocked back the rest of his drink and set the empty glass down on the table. His dark-eyed gaze landed on her as he sat forward. "Well, which one of my daughters are you going to choose?"

Selen paused before she spit out her answer.

As much as she wanted to shout that she wanted Rose, she would not allow him to continue to deceive her. Before coming to the meeting she had placed a quick call to the clan's lawyer to ensure she had a clear and concise under- standing of who was being offered. Tom assured her that she had interpreted it correctly and per the contract it was general—a daughter of the Silver Fang alpha.

"Remind me, Mondo. How many daughters do you have?" she asked. She folded her leg over her other and met his gaze. She felt her bear stand up and lend its strength to her.

Mondo's gaze hardened. He sniffed and rubbed his nose.

"I have four daughters," he answered. He sat straight up and shook his head. "I don't know what you are getting at. You were presented with three of my finest offsprings. Choose one of them."

His tone turned demanding, but Selen wasn't put off by the hint of a threat in his tone. She kept her calm and wits about her. She'd expected for him to act just this way.

"But you say you have four. Why was the fourth not included in the presentation ceremony? The contract clearly states that I am to choose amongst your children."

"Well, you are only getting to chose between the three," he growled.

"Why?" Her voice sliced through the air.

The tension grew thick. Out of the corner of her eye she caught the sight of Nick straightening to his full height. It would only take one word for him to be at her side to defend her. At the moment she didn't need him.

"Listen here, Beta. I don't need to explain myself to you."

"Oh, but you do. The contract stated for me to chose from your daughters, and you, sir, did not present all of them to me. I demand you honor the contract." Selen slowly lowered her leg to the floor. Her bear paced inside her. She kept a close eye on Mondo. The alpha was clearly unused to being questioned. Well, she wasn't from his clan and she had every right to since they had entered an agreement.

"You don't get to make demands—"

"Oh, I do. I'm sure my clan would love to hear how you are trying to deceive—"

"How dare you!" He snarled.

He pushed up from where he stood. Selen

did the same. If he charged at her, she didn't want to be left sitting. Both of the enforcers took a step forward. Selen held up a hand to Nick. The last thing they needed was an all-out brawl.

"How dare I? You have some nerve. Imagine my surprise that the great Mondo Bell would think to offer only three of his four daughters. What do you have to hide?"

She didn't back down from him or look away from the alpha. His chest was rising and falling swiftly. His bear was close to the surface, she could sense it. Hers remained close to the surface as well. Her animal was ready to burst forward to defend her.

"I don't have anything to hide. I made a sound decision to present my most prized daughters to you, and this is what I get? A woman with an attitude and ungrateful. You should be lucky I offered you three strong women. I could have offered anyone to you."

"Why not your fourth daughter?" She arched an eyebrow.

He stalked toward her with a menacing glare. She held her ground, refusing to back down. He stopped directly in froth of her and lowered his head. A growl sounded behind her. She recognized Nick's warning to Mondo.

"What do you know of her? You are asking too much about her," he snarled.

"What's wrong with Rose?" she demanded to know. She wanted him to admit why he treated her mate so differently than the others. She was beautiful, intelligent, kind, and successful. What father wouldn't be proud of a daughter like Rose?

"How do you know her name?" His eyes narrowed on her.

Selen stood firm and rested her hands on her waist. He moved even closer to her and inhaled deeply. His eyes widened suddenly.

He took a step back. "Why is her scent on you?"

"Because she is my mate, and I'm not leaving here without her." Selen's bear gave a rumble of her own. She was so close to the surface that Selen could feel the prickling of her fur scratching at her skin. She fought hard to keep her animal contained. She was ready to fight for her woman. No one would stand in her way when it came to her mate. Not even her father.

"Well, she's not up for negotiation."

"Did I say I was asking? I'm telling you." Selen spun on her heels and headed toward the door.

She couldn't care less about the damn contract. Mondo didn't know who he was up against. Nick had silently made his way a few feet behind her. He gave her a nod and faced the alpha until she was out of the room. The pounding of his footsteps followed behind her. Selen had to contain her rage. Did Mondo think he would be able to stand in the way of fate?

If he thought that, then he had another think coming.

# CHAPTER TWELVE

Rose inhaled sharply and smiled. She could still scent Selen in her cabin. It had been a couple of hours since Selen had left to meet with her father. She was worried about her mate, but Selen had assured her that everything would be taken care of. She had even encouraged Rose to go into town and open her shop as she had planned.

She slid her feet into her shoes before heading to the door. Her car was parked around back. She'd drive today instead of walk. Some days she didn't mind the walk into town. It gave her plenty of opportunities to gather additional herbs on her way into work.

She hummed as she grabbed her keys and her satchel then headed out the front door. She slammed it shut and inserted the key to lock it. Not that she needed to lock her doors, but she was always careful. As a woman living alone, she could never be too careful. Not that Chardon had any crime. No one would dare harm a member of the alpha's family, but there was always the chance that an outsider could be bypassing her cabin and decide to stop by.

Rose froze with her hand on the door. The hairs on the back of her neck stood up slightly. She wasn't alone. She spun around and found her sisters standing in the yard. She took them in, and alarms went off in her head.

"Hey, guys," she said.

She gave a little wave to them, but neither of them cracked a smile. She walked to the edge of her porch. Rose wasn't sure why they were here. She hefted the strap of her bag onto her shoulder.

Her sisters never stopped by her house.

"What did you do?" Harper asked.

Rose blinked. How would her sisters know

about her and Selen already? Were they watching Selen?

"I'm not sure what you are talking about." Rose reached up and tucked her dark hair behind her ear. She erased all emotions from her face to appear innocent. Maybe they were here for some other reason.

Daisy rolled her eyes and folded her arms in front of her.

"Don't play dumb now. We know you are far from it," Daisy muttered.

Well, that was a shock to Rose. Her sisters had never acknowledged her intelligence before. What in the world was going on? Rose shook her head in disbelief. It couldn't be because of Selen. She had only been gone for a couple of hours.

"Seriously. You are scaring me. What's wrong?" Rose asked. She took a step down the stairs. She slid her keys in her back pocket of her jeans. She didn't like the tension in the air.

"I don't think she knows, ladies," Iris murmured. She hadn't taken her eyes off of Rose. She turned to Harper and Daisy. "He wants us to bring her to him."

"Him who?" Rose asked.

Her hands trembled slightly. She closed them

into small fists, not wanting her sisters to see her fear. They were probably already picking up on the aroma of her fear, but she couldn't do anything to mask that. By the looks of them, she wasn't sure she wanted to go anywhere with them.

"Father. He is summoning you," Iris replied, turning back to face Rose.

"Are you coming with us willingly? Or do we need to make you?" Daisy said.

Rose swallowed hard. This was not good. Selen must have already met with her father, and her sisters knew.

That's why they were pissed.

Selen hadn't chosen either of them.

"Why does he need to see me?" Rose asked. If Selen had already met with her father, then where was she? Why hadn't she come back to the cabin? Rose bit her lip. Should she go with her sisters? Was Selen still there?

"She didn't choose any of us," Harper spat. She stalked forward.

Rose scrambled backward up the stairs but tripped. Her bottom hit the top step. A sharp pain rippled through the meat of her ass. She grimaced and glanced up to find Harper standing over her. Rose's bear gave a warning growl.

"She wants you! How? Why?"

Rose's gaze wandered from Harper to Daisy and then over to Iris. She didn't know what else to say but the truth.

"She's my fated mate."

"Like hell she is." Harper snagged Rose's arm and pulled her to her feet.

Her firm grip around her arm caused Rose to wince. Harper stalked away from the cabin and down the path toward the alpha house with the other sisters in tow.

"She is. Why don't you believe me?" Rose cried out. She glanced behind her and saw Iris and Daisy were right behind them.

"When would you have had the chance to meet her?" Daisy snapped.

"Seriously. You didn't even stay for the entire celebration." Iris snorted.

Rose was in absolute shock at the way her sisters were acting. She knew there was a difference between them, but she never would have thought they would act this way toward her. They knew the importance of finding one's mate. Why couldn't they be happy for her? Why didn't they believe her? Did they not think she deserved to find her one true mate?

"But we did meet, and I knew immediately. Actually, I knew before we even met. The moment I first saw her," Rose admitted.

Harper made a hard stop and swung toward Rose who tried to step back away from her sister, but Harper held tight.

"You're telling me that when you first told us what she looked like, you already knew she was your fated mate? The woman we were being presented to?" Harper growled.

Daisy and Iris came to stand next to them. They waited for the answer as well. Rose slowly nodded.

"If you knew, then why didn't you say anything?" Iris demanded.

"This was important to the clan and to you three. Father has spoken nonstop about this agreement and how important forming an alliance with the Brown Claw was for us. That we needed them. He would have had a fit if I would have ruined the chance for one of you to mate with the beta. I-I was willing to sacrifice my happiness for you," she whispered. It would have torn her heart apart to watch one of them with

Selen. She lowered her eyes and exhaled slowly. Her shoulders slumped slightly. Was she going to have to give up Selen still? Was this why her sisters were dragging her off to meet with their father?

To make her give Selen up?

"But why?" This time it was Daisy. Her head tilted to the side as she studied Rose. "Why not be selfish and take what is yours?"

Rose stared at them and shook her head. They really didn't know her. It was sad that they were siblings. They had grown up in the same house with the same parents and they did not truly know her.

"Because this was much bigger than me. Yes, my heart would be broken, but over time it would have healed. The people of our clan mean the world to me, and if one of you mating with Selen would better our clan and our people, then I don't matter." Rose sniffed. Emotions swirled around in her chest. She meant every word she'd said. She had a love for the people of the Silver Fang, and they meant more to her than anything.

Even her own happiness and future.

Harper released a curse and tugged on her arm. "Let's go."

Her sisters led her into the alpha lodge. Even though she had grown up in this home, it suddenly felt different. She felt as if she were being sentenced for a crime she hadn't even committed. Harper marched alongside her while Daisy walked ahead of them and Iris was behind. A few of the house staff stared at them as she was guided through the building. Their whispers filled the air. With her shifter hearing, they might as well speak freely.

*Did she mate with the beta?*

*What is going to happen to her?*

*Why didn't the alpha show off Rose?*

Rose held her head up high as she was escorted to her father's office. She ignored the whispers. It was to no surprise that the staff was already aware that something was going on. Word always spread like wildfire in Chardon. Their small, close-knit town liked to gossip. The house servants were no different.

She hadn't seen any signs of the men who

had traveled with Selen. Had they left? Did her father make her leave?

She swallowed hard.

Had he imprisoned Selen?

Her father did have a temper at times, and honestly, she wouldn't put it past him. They arrived at the double doors to the office. She had been here countless times but never had she been practically dragged there.

Daisy gave a few raps on the door. She glanced over at Rose for a second. The blank expression in her eyes worried Rose. Should she have kept her mouth shut? She wished she could speak with Selen. They hadn't discussed any other outcome than them being together.

"Come in!" her father's deep voice bid them from inside.

Daisy turned the knob and pushed the heavy doors open. Rose swallowed hard as they escorted her inside. Iris shut the door behind them. Her father sat in his oversized leather chair with a brooding expression. She always thought he seemed out of place in his office. Mondo Bell was a gruff-looking man who always appeared wild. He belonged out in the woods and forest. Not behind a desk.

"Father, we have brought you our sister," Harper announced. She pushed Rose forward and released her arm.

Rose immediately began to rub the area where her sister had held on to her. Daisy moved to the side to allow Rose to be front and center.

"Where is she?" Rose blurted out. She glanced around and didn't see anyone there but her siblings and her father. Was Selen harmed? Her bear paced back and forth inside her chest. Worry settled in.

"Don't worry about where she is," Mondo replied.

He stood and rested his hands on the desk. His dark hair fell forward in his face. He combed his fingers through it to push it out of his eyes. His dark eyes, so much like hers, stared back at her. Something passed though them, but she couldn't read what it was.

"Decisions as alpha are never easy. I have an entire clan that depends on me. They expect me to do the right thing."

Rose's heart raced. She didn't know where he was going with this speech, but she really needed him to get to the point. She needed to know if her mate was safe and okay. She held on to the strap of her bag and eyed her father.

"As a father, I have to do the same thing. Make decisions that are best for my family," he continued. He walked around the desk and leaned back against it. He folded his large arms in front of his chest. "None of them have ever been easy."

"Well, there could have been one thing you could have decided," Rose muttered. Her eyes widened at the slip of her tongue. Had she just been cheeky with her father? Her bear snorted and head butted her from the inside. Rose felt the pleasure from her bear. She stood a little straighter. That actually had felt good.

"I don't know where this boldness is coming from or what that beta has done to you, but you watch your tongue," Mondo snapped.

"Why should I?" she demanded. She thumped her fist to her chest. "I am a Bell. The eldest of your daughters. I deserve everything you have ever given them. Why have you always ignored me? Pushed me to the background? What have I done that was so damn wrong to where you don't love me like you love them?"

Her heart was racing a mile a minute. She

was shouting by the time she was done. But she had to know. She had never been so bold to demand he tell her to her face how much she was a disappointment to him. Or why she was lacking. He had always treated her differently.

"Ignored you? I have protected you!" he roared.

Rose shook her head. There was no way that he thought the way he had treated her was protecting her. It had done more damage than good if anything. She blinked back tears.

"Bullshit." There was no way she was backing down now. It was time that she stood up for herself. The question her sister had asked echoed in her head.

*Why not be selfish and take what is yours?*

Well, dammit. She was now. She couldn't care less about the contract and her father's anger. Selen was hers.

"Everything I have done was to protect you. Yes, you are the eldest, but you are the weakest of the—"

"Weakest?" she whispered.

Her eyes widened in shock. She didn't think she could be hurt any more than she had already been. But damn. He saw her as the weakest? It went without saying that he wasn't talking about physical strength. She took a step backward. She glanced over at her sisters and was shocked to see that they stared at their father in horror at his words. Iris glanced over at her with pity filling her eyes.

"Oh, Rose," Iris whispered. She took a step forward to her.

"I think I've heard enough." Rose sniffed. She spun on her heel and raced toward the door.

Her sisters parted and let her through. She snatched open the door and ignored her father shouting her name. She blinked back the tears and raced down the hall. She had to escape and find Selen.

This was it. She didn't care what her father thought. If he felt she was the weakest, her mother probably did as well. Goldie Bell always sided with her mate. There was no reason for Rose to stay in Chardon. She would close her shop up and start over in Lurton with Selen. It may take her a while to get up and running, but she at least would be with someone who wanted her.

Rose raced through the kitchen, surprising the staff. She ignored their stares and headed to the door that led to the veranda. She slid the door open and jogged out of it. She made her way down the stairs. She didn't know where to even start to find Selen. Her bear growled and snapped at her to listen.

She paused in the middle of the property and allowed her bear to lead her.

*Front of the house.*

Rose gripped her bag tight and raced around the building. She wasn't sure why her bear was leading her to the front. She should go home, get her car, and just leave. She turned the corner of and skidded to a halt. The two large SUVs that she'd seen before drove up the driveway and parked.

The back door of the second truck opened, and a beautiful vision stepped from it.

Her mate.

"Selen!" Rose cried out. She took off running toward her.

Selen frowned, her eyes going to the cabin.

"What is it, my love?" Selen asked as Rose's body slammed into hers.

It felt so good to have Selen's strong arms wrapped around her. She pressed a kiss to the top of Rose's head.

"Rose!" her father roared.

Rose stiffened in Selen's arms. She tightened her hold on her and didn't want to turn around to face her father. She glanced up at Selen who was focused on Mondo over Rose's shoulder. She reached down and cupped Rose's cheek, then her eyes met Rose's.

"Don't worry, my love. You are coming home with me."

# CHAPTER THIRTEEN

Selen lowered her eyes and met those of her mate's. The second she had witnessed Rose barreling around the corner of the house, she knew something was wrong. After her confrontation with Mondo, she and her men had packed their belongings and left. She had updated Eddie on what was going on and she had her alpha's full blessing to do what she needed to do in order to secure her mate and take her back to Lurton with her.

"I want you to go to Abe who is standing behind me," Selen murmured. She could feel her men and where they were positioned.

Mondo stalked from the alpha house with his dark eyes narrowed on her and Rose.

"Get your hands off my daughter, Beta. I told you that she was not up for negotiation," he growled.

"And I told you I was not asking for your permission to claim my fated mate," Selen snapped. Her bear was rising to the surface fast. She gently moved Rose off to the side to place her behind her.

"No. He's too strong for you," Rose cried out softly.

She tried to remain in front of Selen, but Selen was still able to move her out of the way. Mondo's fangs were out, and his fur was rippling along his skin.

A growl rumbled from her. Her bear decided it was time for her to come out. There was no way Mondo was going to keep her from Rose.

"Abe," Selen snapped.

Her enforcer scooped up Rose and took her to safety. Selen would need to concentrate, and she wouldn't be able to do that if she was worried her mate would be in the line of danger. Her fangs burst through her gums. The change was coming, and she was not going to prevent it.

Her bear would do what she must to protect their mate. The other Bell sisters stumbled out of the lodge along with others trailing behind them. Selen recognized Mondo's enforcers rushing out of the doors.

She wasn't worried. Her men would not allow them to interfere between her and the alpha.

"You want to defy me on my land! In front of my people, then you will pay, Beta," Mondo growled just before his bear burst forth. His body doubled in size as the change took hold of him. His body molded and contorted while his clothes fell to the ground in shreds.

Selen turned herself over completely to her animal and allowed her beast to come out. Her body was swift in shifting. She fell to the ground on all fours once her bear was completely out.

She threw her head back and let loose a powerful roar. Just because she wasn't an alpha didn't mean she wasn't strong enough to take one on. She blinked and focused on the oversized bear staring at her. Selen brandished her fangs to show that she wasn't afraid of Mondo. A small crowd was forming. They walked toward each other.

Selen's bear was in a rage. She was free, and before her stood the man—bear—who was going to try to keep their mate from them. Mondo's bear charged at her. The ground shook from his weight. Selen was not going to back down. Her bear was ready for the fight. She planted her feet on the ground and was ready.

His large form came barreling at her. She sidestepped him and swung her mighty paw at him. Her large talons made contact with his side. She drew the first blood. He roared and spun on his heel to face her again. This time he stood on his hind legs. He towered easily over her. She did the same, showcasing she was not afraid of him.

Another roar filled the air. A smaller bear came rushing toward them and skidded to a halt between she and Mondo.

Rose.

Selen growled. She didn't want her mate to get hurt in the fight. Rose's bear was not backing down from her father. He growled and shook his paws as if to tell her to move.

But Rose was not heeding her father.

She stood on her hind legs in front of Selen. It would appear her mate was trying to protect her, but Selen didn't need Rose shielding her.

Selen fell down to all fours in shock that her mate was willing to put herself between her and the alpha.

*Rose! Move!* she tried to shout, but in her bear form it came out as a series of grunts and growls.

Rose's bear was fierce and was not backing down from her father. She advanced on Mondo. He took steps back, and it would appear he wouldn't fight his daughter. Selen was proud of her, but they would be having a long conversation later.

Her mate was to never get between her and a foe.

Selen didn't care that it was her father. There was no telling how Mondo would have reacted. Selen moved to stand beside Rose. Her gaze was locked on Mondo. His dark eyes flicked between the two of them. He backed away. Rose continued forward, growling low.

The air around Mondo shimmered. He shifted back into his human form. He knelt on the ground and raised a hand to Rose. He focused on his daughter.

"Rose! Shift," he ordered.

The alpha waves that burst from him were strong. It sent a rippling current through the air.

His power slammed into Selen and caused her to take a step back. The other shifters standing around were almost knocked to the ground.

Rose roared again. She stood on her hind legs in defiance. She was a magnificent bear with her dark-brown fur, long talons, and sharp fangs. Selen had a hard time tearing her eyes away from her mate.

"I said shift," Mondo shouted again.

He stood to his full height, but Rose was not listening to her father. She was too far in her rage, and her bear was in complete control.

Selen decided to change back as well. Her bear at first resisted the change. Rose was in her bear form, and her animal wanted to stay out. Her bear whined as she continued to look at Rose.

*We must help our mate,* Selen whispered to her beast. Her animal continued to hesitate but then decided to listen to Selen. The fur along her skin retreated, and her body morphed back into her human form. She opened her eyes and lifted her gaze to find Rose's bear still standing there.

"Rose," Selen called to her.

Her bear's head snapped around, and her gaze landed on Selen. She took a step toward her with her palms facing the bear. There was no fear in her heart of the bear before her. The only fear she had was what Mondo would do if Rose actually did attack her father. If he so much as laid a hand on her, he would answer to Selen.

"Shift, my love. Come back to me."

Confusion filled Rose's eyes. She looked over at her father for a brief moment before turning back to Selen.

"It's okay, my love. Give me back my Rose," Selen said.

She went to stand before Rose. She reached out a hand and ran it along the center of the bear's chest which rose and fell fast. Selen didn't like seeing her mate so worked up and angry. She should leave that to Selen.

"Give me my Rose."

Rose snorted and fell down to all fours. The air shimmered when she gave herself over to the change. Her body shifted, her bones shortening, the fur receding into her skin. Within a minute, she was kneeling on the ground. Her dark hair fell forward like a curtain, hiding her face.

"Baby, are you okay?" Selen asked. She knelt down beside her and rested her hands on her shoulders. They were trembling underneath her touch. Selen didn't give a damn who was watching. All she wanted to do was make sure her mate was okay.

Rose lifted her head. Her hair fell away to reveal her beautiful face. Her eyes were bloodshot as if she had been crying. She reached up and took Selen's hand in hers.

"Of course I am."

They stood together, both naked after their shift. Selen eyed her and didn't see any injuries. Not that her father would have been able to get close to her. Selen would never allow that to happen.

"Don't ever get between me and someone else like that—"

"I couldn't let you face him alone," Rose interrupted. She turned to Selen and cupped her face with her hands. Her eyes softened, and a small smile came to her lips. "You are my mate, and we will face everything together."

How could Selen stay mad at her? At the moment her heart melted. They would still have a long conversation when it was just the two of them, but for now, they still had to deal with her father. As if remembering he and other members from her clan were watching them, Rose turned to her father.

"Selen is my fated mate," Rose announced. She stood proudly and entwined her fingers with Selen's. "I don't care about a contract. No one should ever miss the opportunity to be with the one that fate made for them."

"Rose," Mondo said.

He stepped forward, but she held up a hand.

"I'm not done, Father. I know I am not the strongest daughter, nor can I make weapons or sing as beautiful as my sisters, but I'm me. I'm Rose. Your eldest. I'm smart and I help people when they are sick. I demand respect, and if you cannot give me that, then I will no longer be your daughter."

The tension in the air could have been cut with a knife. Selen was shocked at her words. She decided to remain silent. She squeezed Rose's hand to lend her strength.

"You will always be my daughter," Mondo said. He swallowed hard, and at that moment, uncertainty entered his eyes.

"Then you need to start treating me like you do my sisters," Rose demanded. She pushed her hair from her face.

Selen stood in awe of her. She had a feeling Rose had never stood up to her father before.

"She is right," a voice said from behind the crowd.

It parted and revealed Goldie, Rose's mother. She walked forward and stopped next to her husband. She glanced over at Rose with sadness in her eyes. "Too long has there been a divide in our family, Mondo. I've sat by and have not said a word. But no longer. It ends today. Fix this. If they are fated mates, then who are we to stand in their way?"

Mondo stared down at his wife, and immediately the rest of the fight left him. He gave a nod to Goldie. It was easy to see that the two of them were meant for each other. The moment Goldie had come to his side and spoken, he'd listened to her. Mondo stood to his full height and faced Selen and Rose.

"If you are willing to, we can go back to the negotiations. I will give my blessings on your mating with our daughter, Rose."

The crowd cheered. Rose turned to Selen and threw herself in her arms. Selen squeezed her tight. Rose tilted her head up toward Selen, and she didn't hesitate to claim her lips in a short, hard kiss. She leaned her forehead on Rose's and smiled.

"How about it, my love? Want me to sign a contract for our mating?" Selen asked, her voice soft.

Rose's beautiful face lit up brightly.

"There is no one else for you but me, so you better sign it," Rose replied, haughty.

Selen barked a laugh. She didn't know where this feisty version of Rose had come from, but she loved it. Selen gathered her close to her side and turned back to the alpha couple. They made their way to Rose and Selen with Rose's sisters right behind them.

"I'd be honored to negotiate for our two clans as long as Rose is my designated mate."

# EPILOGUE

Rose walked around her new store and was in awe. Rose's Apothecary was officially going to open in Lurton. It had been six months since her father and Selen had signed the contract to join their two clans as allies. Rose still could not believe how she had stood up to her father. Her bear had always been protective of her, but that day, her bear was not going to let her father get the best of her or harm Selen.

The relationship between her and her family was slowly on the mend. It wasn't going to be something that was fixed overnight, but she was happy that they were going in the right direction.

Selen had been a huge support with everything. With the move to Lurton and expanding her business. She had hired a couple of local women from Chardon to run her store while she got the Lurton store off the ground. She would travel back and forth when needed.

Since moving to Lurton, she had been welcomed with open arms. So many members of the Brown Claw had come to her and Selen's home that it was going to take her a minute to learn everyone's name. Excitement had filled the town when it had been announced that she was opening a second shop.

Tomorrow was the big day for her Lurton location. It was small just like the one in Chardon and it was just what she needed. Pride filled her that she had expanded. She had always dreamed of doing so, and with Selen's support, she was able to. It was in the middle of town and was next to a cute ice cream shop called the Lick & Bite. The building was newly renovated and was perfect for her store.

Rose paused in front of one of her displays of teas. A box was out of place. She gently slid it back where it belonged and stepped back. The display was now perfect.

Life here was going amazing. She had been worried about traveling back and forth between the two towns, but it was seamless. She still kept her cabin in Chardon. Her mother had a cleaning lady come once a week to ensure it was well kept.

The ringing of the phone snagged her attention. She jogged over behind the counter and answered it.

"Rose's Apothecary," she said.

"Hi, are you open yet?" a warm voice asked.

"Not yet. The grand opening is to tomorrow at ten a.m.," Rose said. A smile spread across her face. This was the third call she'd received today with the same question. It would seem the residents of Lurton were looking forward to the new shop in town.

"Well, I will see you then. Thanks!"

Rose giggled as she hung up. She was so excited for tomorrow. They were planning a small reception with drinks and snacks to welcome the first customers. She did another sweep through of the store and found everything to be in perfect shape. She had ensured the vibe of the shop was welcoming with warm colors and soft music playing.

A knock sounded. She moved to the front of the store and saw her mate standing outside with a bag in her hand.

Rose hurried over to the door and opened it.

"Hey, you. I was wondering when you were going to show up." Rose laughed.

Selen stepped in and shut the door behind her. She immediately went into her welcoming embrace. Selen's soft lips covers hers in a slow, passionate kiss. Rose's knees went weak, and she melted against her. They finally came up for air, and it was then that she scented the contents of the bag.

"What's in here?"

She wrapped her arms around Selen's waist, not ready to let her go.

"I stopped and grabbed us a bite to eat. I figured you'd want to stay here and make sure everything is ready for tomorrow," Selen said.

"You know me so well." Rose smiled.

She entwined her fingers with Selen's and led her to the back where her office was. They could eat their supper there before finishing off last-minute tasks that she wanted to conquer before going home.

"That I do," Selen murmured.

She trailed behind Rose. When they crossed over the threshold of Rose's tiny office, she wrapped her arms around Rose's stomach and pulled her back to her. She propped their food on Rose's desk before nuzzling her face into the crook of Rose' neck. "I missed you."

Rose moaned at the feel of Selen's lips sliding along her sensitive skin. The food was suddenly forgotten as her body came to life under her touch. Selen's hand slipped underneath her t-shirt and caressed her belly. Rose spun around in her embrace and raised her arms. She brought Selen's head down to hers and offered up her lips.

There wasn't a day that went by that Rose didn't feel loved. Her mate had ensured that she never felt alone, unloved, or forgotten.

"Not hungry right now?" Selen broke the kiss and smiled down at Rose.

Rose grinned at her. She was still hungry, but the food could wait. They could always heat it up when they got home. She reached down and captured the edge of Selen's shirt and brought it over her head. She tossed it on the floor behind her and walked her backwards until she was met by Rose's desk.

"Actually, I am very hungry, but not for food."

Her fingers went to Selen's jeans and pulled the button open. They both worked together to slide them and her panties down. Selen's long, tan legs were beautiful. She sat on the table and moved their food out of the way, placing it on Rose's chair. She grinned and helped her open her legs. Her gaze found Selen's slick center. Her swollen pink clit was calling Rose. She licked her lips and slid a finger through Selen's folds. The wetness that coated her finger made her core clench.

Right now she was going to have her dessert first.

Dinner could definitely wait.

# ABOUT THE AUTHOR

Ariel Marie is an author who loves the paranormal, action and hot steamy romance. She combines all three in each and every one of her stories. For as long as she can remember, she has loved vampires, shifters and every creature you can think of. This even rolls over into her favorite movies. She loves a good action packed thriller! Throw a touch of the supernatural world in it and she's hooked!

*Sign up for Ariel Marie's newsletter!*
*Scan the QR Code to get all the latest news from Ariel Marie!*

*For more information visit:*
www.thearielmarie.com

## The Nightstar Shifters

**No wolf can resist the call to mate.**

Strong female wolves are in search of their mate. The desire is strong for these women who long to find the one person meant for them.

They are fierce and determined, putting their trust in fate.

*If you love lesbian wolf shifter romance filled with action and adventure, then you will love the Nightstar Shifters series.*

*Ready to start the Nightstar Shifters? Click HERE to download book one!*

# The Immortal Reign Series

*Vampires and Humans. Are they meant to be together? One drop of blood will control their futures.*

After the war between vampires and humankind, Earth was never the same. This new world was dangerous, and vampires were on the hunt for their fated mates. The installation of the draft should have made things simpler, but all it did was create chaos.

Humans didn't want to conform to the new ways of life.

Vampires had no problems making them.

*Enter this new dark and sexy world full of lesbian vampire romance. The Immortal Reign series is an adult-themed paranormal romance that you will want to sink your teeth into. If you love action-packed, sizzling hot wlw romances, then this is the series for you.*

*Start the Immortal Reign series today! Click HERE to download book one!*

# ALSO BY ARIEL MARIE

Nicu